NANTUCKET NEIGHBORS

PAMELA M. KELLEY

PIPING PLOVER PRESS

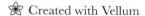

INTRODUCTION

Book your visit to the Beach Plum Cove Inn today.....meet widow Lisa Hodges and her four adult children, friends, and visitors to the newly opened waterfront bed and breakfast. In the first book, The Nantucket Inn, Lisa learned that her deceased husband had a hidden gambling addiction and had blown through their retirement savings. Since she'd been raising four children and hadn't worked in years, she had no employable skills. Her only option if she wanted to stay on the island near her loved ones, was to rent out her second floor rooms.

And she's loving it so far. Lisa's first guest, restaurant owner Rhett Byrne quickly became a close friend and then something more. In her early fifties, it sounds strange to her to call him her boyfriend, but that's what he is.

Her daughter Kristen, finally ended things with Sean, the separated man that no one in the family was excited about. It wasn't until she was beginning to move on, that he filed for divorce, and then begged her for another chance. So she gave him one, much to everyone's dismay. But then the cottage next door is sold, and she discovers who her new neighbor is.

Chase, the only boy in the family, has never been serious about anyone before. But he's suddenly withdrawn and has been secretive about who he's seeing, which only makes everyone that much more curious. When they learn who it is, the concern grows as no one wants to see Chase hurt, again.

Lisa's best friend, Paige, has a new neighbor too and it's one she is most decidedly not enthused about. Violet was one of the women who stood up at town meeting and protested against Lisa's inn being approved by the selectman. Because the house is right next door, Paige can't help but notice the steady stream of traffic. Violet seems to be very popular with a lot of people.

The inn is doing well and bookings are up, but then one Friday night, a guest that prepaid for the weekend never shows up. And quite a few people, including the police, come asking questions.

L isa Hodges walked along the empty beach and breathed in deeply as a soft gust of wind blew her hair across her face. The steady boom of the waves crashing against the sand soothed her soul. It was one of her favorite sounds. She loved these early morning walks when she had the beach, and her thoughts all to herself.

She picked up her pace when a glance at her phone showed the time. She wanted to be back to the house by a quarter of eight, to be ready for her first guests. Breakfast started at eight and Rhett, her very first guest--the one who came and never left--was usually there right at eight. She joined him most days, and when her girls came to visit, they did too. She smiled as she thought of Rhett. It seemed silly, at her age, almost fifty-four, to say that she had a boyfriend, but that's what Rhett had become, much to her surprise.

Rhett was a few years older than Lisa and was on Nantucket to open his newest restaurant. His original plan had been to move into a rental, but he decided to stay long term at the Beach Plum Cove Inn instead, and Lisa was enjoying his company immensely. They went out to eat at least once a week and she had him over for dinner often too.

It was funny how things sometimes worked out. When her husband of over thirty years died several years ago, Lisa had been dismayed to learn that he'd blown through most of their retirement savings. She'd felt foolish that she hadn't realized his occasional casino trips with his buddies, was really a gambling addiction. But Brian had been a financial advisor, and she'd always trusted him to handle their finances.

Lisa had tried unsuccessfully to find work locally, but since she hadn't worked in years, she had no employable skills and no way to support herself if she stayed. The situation was so dire that Lisa was faced with only two options--sell the house and move off-island away from her family and friends--or try to turn her large waterfront home into a bed-and-breakfast. Since their area of the island was called Beach Plum Cove, she decided on the name The Beach Plum Cove Inn.

Her son Chase had helped her do the minor renovating that was necessary, basically to just close off the downstairs by adding a wall. There were five rooms upstairs, each with their own bath, and every morning she served breakfast in the dining room, the only room guests had access to during breakfast hours.

So far, the inn was doing better than Lisa had expected. She really hadn't known what to expect, but thanks to Airbnb and some online advertising her daughter Kate had set up for her, The Beach Plum Cove Inn was steady with bookings, which was a relief.

When she reached the house, she saw that all three of her girls had arrived. Kate was filling a big thermos with coffee while Kristen was arranging cut fruit on a platter. Abby, her youngest, was sitting at the island, patting her stomach. She was almost four months pregnant now and just starting to show, but only if you looked closely. Kate handed Abby a mug of coffee and she proceeded to dump four sugars into it.

"Are you feeling okay?" Lisa couldn't help but worry about her youngest daughter and her future grandchild, the first in the family.

Abby smiled as she lifted her coffee mug to take a sip. "I'm feeling a lot better, actually. I'm not as tired now and the morning sickness has eased up a bit. The mad cravings have started though."

"Oh? For what kind of things?" Kate asked.

Abby laughed. "Fried clams. Isn't that the strangest thing? I want them at least once a week now, and vanilla ice cream almost every day. Though that's not all that unusual."

"What were your cravings, Mom?" Kristen asked.

Lisa thought for a moment. "Definitely ice cream, that was for all of them and chocolate for you girls. With Chase, I craved potato chips and red meat. I always wanted either steak or meatballs."

Abby looked interested. "They say if you crave salty things you're having a boy. I thought it was an old wives tale, but that was true for you."

Lisa shrugged. "Maybe. Though these days I think I'd rely more on what an ultrasound says."

"True. Ultrasounds are sometimes wrong though, the early ones anyway. Jeff is looking forward to having the next one and having this confirmed. I'll hold off on decorating until then. "

Kate asked the question they'd all been wondering about. "How is he doing? Are things still going well with his work hours?" Abby had been so frustrated with the long hours Jeff worked that she'd considered divorce, even after finding out she was pregnant. They seemed to be working through it and Lisa hoped that Jeff wouldn't slide back into his old habits.

"So far so good. He's actually been great lately. He's excited about the baby."

"Good." Lisa grabbed two potholders and took a quiche out of the oven. She'd put it in to warm up while she went on her walk. "Let's head into the dining room with everything. Rhett should be down any minute."

They brought the food into the dining room and set it on the counter so everyone could help themselves. Lisa was starving after her walk and cut herself a generous wedge of ham and red pepper quiche. Abby and Kate did the same and Kristen just put a little fruit on a plate and nibbled at it while the rest of them ate.

"Something smells good." Lisa's favorite guest, Rhett Byrne, walked into the room and helped himself to a cup of coffee and then settled next to her at the dining room table. He liked to ease into his day and always had one cup of coffee before getting anything to eat. He was her only guest at the moment, though they were booked solid for the rest of the weekend.

"Any movie news?" Rhett asked Kate. Kate had recently published her first mystery and thanks to an introduction from local celebrity author, Philippe Gaston, her book had been optioned by a famous brother-sister team.

"Not a peep. Though Philippe said that's normal, and he warned me that it might never actually get out of the option stage, but I'm optimistic. They both really seemed excited about it."

"It's a good story, would make a great movie," Rhett said.

Kate looked shocked. "You read it?"

"He read the first few pages of my copy a few days ago and I offered to lend it to him, but he insisted on buying his own." Lisa had thought that was sweet but unnecessary.

"Of course I did. I wanted my own copy, and she doesn't earn anything if I borrow yours."

"Well, that's true." He did have a point. Lisa hadn't considered that. Until recently, Kate had worked as a writer for Boston Style magazine. But when the company was sold, she was one of many that were laid off. She still did some freelance work for them, but since moving home to Nantucket, she'd turned her attention to writing mystery novels. And so far, it was going better than expected.

"Has anyone heard from Chase this week? I left him a message a few days ago and haven't heard a peep back yet." Lisa wasn't really worried, but Chase usually was better about calling her back.

"I talked to him briefly a few days ago. I caught him as he was heading out the door and he said he'd call me back. But he hasn't yet. He also didn't mention where he was going," Abby said. If anyone knew what Chase was up to, it would be Abby. The two of them had a bond similar to the one twins Kate and Kristen, shared.

"I bet there's a girl involved and for some reason he doesn't want to talk about it yet. Which might mean he thinks we won't approve," Kristen said.

"Or maybe he just wants to keep it to himself for a while. Until he knows that it's going to go somewhere," Abby suggested.

"Well, I won't worry then, since you've talked to him. I think I'll have a bit more quiche." Lisa cut herself a sliver and didn't feel at all guilty about it. She'd been good about getting in her daily walks and eating healthier.

"Have you met your new neighbor yet?" Lisa asked Kristen as she sat back down. "I noticed the sold sign is gone." Kristen lived in a charming small cottage that had a lovely sunroom and a studio area where she did her painting. The cottage next door was identical in size and design and had recently gone on the market and sold in record time. Anything that was reasonably priced was snatched up quickly on Nantucket, where most homes went for well over a million dollars.

"No, I haven't yet. Though I saw a moving van there yesterday. I haven't heard a peep though, so whoever is there is quiet so far, thankfully." Before the house was sold, it had been used as a summer rental and some of the college kids that stayed there had been annoyingly loud, with late night parties.

"Do you have any shows coming up soon, honey?" Lisa asked. Kristen occasionally showed her paintings at local galleries, but she wasn't very aggressive about getting out there and networking.

Kristen grimaced. "No, I don't. I should probably reach out to Andrew and a few of the other galleries to see about setting something up or just getting some of my newer stuff out on commission."

"Have you talked to Andrew lately?" Lisa was curious. She'd been relieved when Kristen finally ended things with Sean, the man she'd been dating for too long. He'd been separated when they met and never took the next step to file for divorce. When Kristen went on a date with Andrew, the new gallery owner, Lisa had been thrilled. But it never got off the ground. When Sean realized Kristen was serious about ending things, he finally filed for divorce and begged her to take him back. And she did.

"No, I haven't. Not since I got back together with Sean."

"How is that going?" Abby asked her.

Kristen was quiet for a moment before simply saying, "It's fine. We're going to that big charity event at his golf club tonight." But Lisa noticed there was no spark of joy in her eyes. She hurt for her daughter and wanted her to find happiness, but knew she needed to figure it out for herself.

Kate jumped in to change the subject, "I was tweaking our Facebook ads and set up a new campaign to run through the next few months."

"Thanks, honey."

"I took a look at the reservations calendar before I updated the ads and I thought I saw that you had someone that was supposed to be checking in last night. A Tom Smith, I think? It looked like he paid in full too."

Lisa frowned. "He did yes. It's the strangest thing, actually. He never checked in."

"Maybe he missed the last boat?" Kristen said. It was certainly possible.

"Could be. I'm sure he'll show up today. He's paid through Sunday." Lisa would refund him for the night that he missed. She knew that she didn't need to, but it didn't seem right to keep it, especially if the poor guy did miss the boat.

"Do not refund him," Kate said, almost as if she'd read her mother's mind.

Lisa laughed. "We'll see. Let's just hope he shows up today."

2

B*e careful what you wish for*.....the thought occurred to Kristen Hodges not for the first time as she leaned against the large bedroom window and breathed in the cool, slightly salty air. Sean was taking forever to get ready, and she hated the dress she was wearing. The fabric was stiff and a bit itchy and the sleeveless, low-cut neckline was not her style, at all. But Sean had given her the dress as a gift and he was so excited about it that it was just easier to wear it and pretend that she liked it too.

"What are you doing? Finish getting ready or we're going to be late." The irritation in his voice was evident.

Kristen closed the window and turned around to face him. "I'm ready. I'm just waiting on you." Her tone was light and teasing, but Sean frowned as he looked her up and down.

"The dress looks great, but you don't look finished. Why don't you put on that necklace I gave you and the matching earrings?" Another of his gifts, also not her style. But, the diamond necklace and drop earrings were pretty, just much larger and more obvious than she would ever have chosen for herself. Not that she could have ever afforded them, anyway. But they would go well with the dress.

"That's a good idea," she agreed and went to put the jewelry on, while Sean went back to adding gel to his hair. It helped to hide the gray, though lately there was more than he could totally get rid of. She thought it made him look distinguished, but he was horrified and said he was going to make an appointment soon for someone to take care of it.

Sean was a good looking man. Even at almost fifteen years her senior, he looked younger and was in good shape, except for his middle which was getting a little soft lately. He liked to indulge in fine dining and accompanying wines or cocktails. Like the rest of her family, he considered himself a 'foodie'. Kristen enjoyed a good meal, but it wasn't a priority like it was with the rest of them. Her sisters often teased her about her propensity to miss meals entirely when she was caught up in a day of painting. They couldn't understand how it was possible to forget to eat, but she'd often lose all track of time.

She was looking forward to the dinner at tonight's event though. While the people might be stuffy, she'd always enjoyed the food at Sean's fancy club. It was an exclusive country club, with the newest golf course on the island and joining fees that were rumored to be seven figures. Sean liked people to think he'd paid that, but he confessed to Kristen that he'd negotiated a free membership when he brokered the sale of the land. He was very good at what he did and was among the top real estate brokers on the island. Nantucket was a lucrative market where even small homes typically sold for well over a million and many close to ten million or higher.

Kristen had never cared much about that though—money and power weren't attractive to her. She'd met Sean several years ago when he wandered into a small art gallery where she was having a show, her first solo show actually and she'd been equally nervous and excited. As it was winding down, Sean showed up and bought her favorite painting. They'd chatted a bit and there was an instant connection.

He'd just separated from his wife and there was a sadness and a vulnerability about him at the time that touched her. He hadn't tried to impress her either, maybe sensing correctly that it wouldn't have worked.

Instead, he'd asked her to go for a walk after the show ended and they'd ended up talking for hours and then getting takeout sandwiches and eating them on the beach while they watched the sun set and both sensed that something special was beginning.

There were still glimpses of that Sean now and then. He showed up just often enough that she missed him when he wasn't around. At first, their relationship was almost perfect as Kristen had always been somewhat casual and independent with relationships--she liked to keep things light, and not too serious as her focus was always on her painting.

Most guys she'd dated had always pushed her for more of a commitment which was usually when she ended things. But Sean was different. And as time went on, for the first time, she began to crave more of a commitment, and more of his time. She'd assumed that he'd be divorced within a year or two, but he kept pushing off filing, always saying it was 'complicated' and that the timing wasn't right.

She understood it, to a point—Sean had lots of financial holdings, properties and other investments that would need untangling and he had a child too, a teenage son, Julian. So, she'd never pushed until the past year when he still hadn't filed and was regularly canceling on her at the last minute to spend time with his son and ex-wife.

It wasn't until she reached her breaking point, ended the relationship and actually went on a date with someone new-- that Sean finally came to his senses. He filed for divorce and begged Kristen to take him back. And because he'd finally done what she'd been asking for, she felt as though she needed to give their relationship a second chance.

"Now you look ready to go!" Sean flashed her the smile that used to make her heart skip a beat. She was glad that he seemed to be in a better mood. She followed him out to his sleek silver Mercedes. It was a leased sedan, and just a few months old. He traded them in as soon as his lease ended so that he always had something shiny and new. The contrast between his showy car and her practical, ten-year-old Honda Civic was stark. She climbed into the passenger side and relaxed against the buttery black leather while Sean drove the short distance to the club.

When they were almost there, she felt her phone vibrate and glanced down to see a text message from Kate that made her smile.

Philippe had to fly to L.A. unexpectedly and gave Jack and I his tickets. So we'll see you tonight.

Good. She was relieved that her sister would be there. Sean would be in his networking glory, wanting to work the room and chat with all the important people and she'd been dreading having to make small talk with strangers.

When they pulled up to the front door of the sprawling, gray-shingled country club, a young man, one of the many valets, stood waiting to open her door. A moment later, Sean handed over his keys and they went inside. They followed the other new arrivals to the function room, which Kristen had to admit, was lovely. It was huge and decorated in soft blue-gray and creamy white. One wall was almost entirely floor to ceiling windows with sweeping ocean views.

There were at least a hundred and fifty or maybe even close to two hundred people already and there was a buzz of energy as people greeted old friends and new ones they hoped to impress.

"Chardonnay?" Sean asked as they made their way toward one of several bars along the sides of the room.

Kristen nodded yes as a handsome server holding a silver tray, stopped to offer mini-crab cakes and scallops wrapped in bacon. She took two scallops and offered one to Sean when he returned with her wine.

"No, you have it. I see someone I need to go talk to for a minute. You'll be okay?"

"Of course. Kate and Jack should be here any minute."

Surprise flashed across his face. "Oh, I didn't know they were coming."

"It was a last-minute thing." She popped the other scallop in her mouth as Sean ran off to stalk his prey. Kristen sipped her chardonnay and glanced around the room, recognizing many faces, but not knowing any of them well enough to go talk to them. All of Nantucket's important people were there, as Sean had expected.

Many of them owned businesses on the island, or had second homes and worked in Boston or New York City, flying in on weekends,—many on their own private planes. Kristen had often watched from Sean's side as these people talked to each other. She saw them size each other up and the talk always turned to what they did, what kind of business they owned, where they lived. Many owned palatial homes on Nantucket but rarely visited more than a few weeks a year. It had always seemed like such a waste to Kristen, to have these big, beautiful homes sitting empty most of the year. Most didn't even rent them out, so others could enjoy them.

"Where's Sean?" Kristen turned at the sound of her sister Kate's voice. She and Jack had just arrived and found the bar before making their way over to her. Jack was holding a beer and Kate had a glass of white wine too. She was so glad that they'd been able to come.

"He's off talking to someone. Said he'd be right

back, but I'm not holding my breath. You know how he is at these things."

Kate smiled. "He's working the room. I imagine there are a lot of potential commissions here."

"That's true. And he's so busy lately. He hired two new brokers this week and is taking over the space of the office next door."

Jack whistled softly. "On Main Street? That's not cheap." He was right, Main Street rents were crazy expensive and when Sean told her what the new amount would be, her jaw had dropped. She just couldn't wrap her head around paying so much. But he wasn't the least bit concerned. She turned her attention to Kate and Jack.

"You look gorgeous, as always. Is that a new dress?" Kristen asked.

"Thanks. It is new. I bought it in Boston right before I moved home." Her sister was wearing a cherry red dress with delicate spaghetti straps that showed off her tanned, toned arms. Kate had always been tall and slim and lately, she'd been glowing with happiness. Ever since she and Jack got together.

When Kate moved home just before Christmas, she'd been through a bad breakup and the last thing she was looking for was another relationship. But when she'd moved into her mother's best friend, Paige's house for the winter, Jack lived just a few doors down and had also recently ended a relation-ship. They started spending time together and now, Kristen couldn't imagine them apart. They made it look easy, but she suspected that when it was right, it was easier.

"You look lost in thought," Kate teased her as Jack walked off to say hello to a friend, and Kristen realized she'd done exactly that. She'd been doing it a lot lately, thinking about what she was doing with Sean and how much longer she was going to do it for.

"I have some decisions to make soon," she admitted.

Kate nodded, understanding what she meant. "You know how I feel about it. Let me know if I can do anything to help." Kate had made it clear that she felt Kristen could do better, much better.

"Thanks."

"Is that Chase? Did you know he was coming tonight? This isn't his kind of thing at all."

Kristen followed her sister's gaze, and was just as surprised to see their younger brother there, looking tall and handsome in a suit neither of them had seen before and talking to a very pretty girl with long blonde hair. She was wearing a sleek white slip dress and impossibly high pink heels. There was another man with them, and they were both laughing at something he said.

"No, it's not," Kristen agreed. "Do you know who that is?"

Kate squinted and cocked her head, thinking. "I'm not a hundred percent sure, but maybe it's that girl Abby said she saw him with at The Chicken Box—Lauren something or other.

Chase turned, as if he sensed their eyes on him and smiled when he saw his sisters. He said something to the other two and made his way over to talk to them. He grinned as he reached them.

"I bet you're surprised to see me here."

"That's an understatement," Kate agreed.

"Lauren and her brother had tickets. They always come to these kinds of things. I told her it wasn't really my scene, but she asked so nicely that it was hard to say no."

"And you bought a new suit and everything. You must really like her?" Kristen couldn't remember the last time she'd seen her brother in a suit. He was a self-employed building contractor, so jeans and a t-shirt was much more his style.

Chase looked somewhat embarrassed. "Lauren is cool. She helped me pick out the suit, said it was a good investment and that I'd have it for years."

"So, tell us about her. How long have you been dating? Will you introduce us?"

He nodded. "Of course. She's on her way over

now." Lauren walked to his side and Chase put his arm around her and pulled her slightly into him.

"Lauren, I'd like you to meet my sisters, Kristen and Kate."

"Nice to meet you," they said at the same time and then laughed. As twins, they'd often done that.

Lauren smiled and then glanced around the room. Kristen followed her gaze and noticed Lauren's brother talking to Sean and neither man looked happy. When Lauren turned her attention back to them, Kristen could see why her brother was so captivated. She was a gorgeous girl, with sleek straight blond hair that fell in a sharp, bob to her shoulders, clear blue eyes and delicate, pretty features. She was petite and had a trim figure with toned arms that looked as though she worked out regularly. Kristen wondered what they had in common as Lauren seemed more sophisticated than the girls her brother usually dated.

"You work in real estate too?" Kristen asked as a way to make conversation.

Lauren's face lit up, and she looked curious. "I do, yes, do you? Chase didn't mention that anyone in his family was into real estate."

"Oh, no! I'm an artist. My boyfriend, Sean, is into real estate. You probably know him, Sean Prescott.

Lauren's face clouded as Kristen felt a light hand on her shoulder.

"Did someone call?" Sean teased. He looked around the group, nodded at Chase and smiled. "Nice to see you Lauren. I was just chatting with your brother. He said you're doing a great job, fantastic for just a new agent."

Lauren seemed to bristle at the implication that she was new.

"It's been several years now and things are going well, thanks." She turned to Chase. "I see someone I need to go say hello to. I'll catch up with you in a bit."

"Are you having fun?" Sean asked her and then greeted the others. "Kate, Jack, good to see you both. I'm sure Kristen was glad to see you. She hates these things."

Kristen laughed. "I don't hate them. Hate's a strong word."

"Well, you'd probably rather be home with your painting?"

"Generally, yes. But, you're right, I'm glad my family is here tonight, makes it more fun."

"Good. Speaking of fun, I see someone I need to go talk to. You don't mind do you?"

"Of course not. Go mingle."

Kristen laughed at the expression on her sister's face as Sean walked away.

"I've never understood what you see in him. He's the last person I would have picked for you. I did hope that things would be better for you since he finally filed for divorce though?"

Kristen didn't really want to talk about it yet though, not even with her sister. Not until she was sure of what she was going to do. She ignored the question and changed the subject.

"You should try one of the scallops in bacon, they're delicious." Kristen reached for another as a server stopped and held out a silver tray full of appetizers. She grabbed a stuffed mushroom too.

They spent the next few hours chatting and enjoying the food. Sean joined them when dinner was about to be served and they were seated at a round table with several other people that both Sean and Jack knew.

Jack Trattel ran his family's seafood business, which supplied many of the local restaurants on the island, so it seemed that he knew almost as many people as Sean did. But the difference between them was night and day. While Sean was on the prowl, roaming the room and seeking out people to talk to, Jack mostly stayed by Kate's side and politely chatted with anyone who stopped by to say hello.

After dinner, there was dancing and a dessert table along one wall. Kristen and Kate helped themselves while Sean excused himself to go chat with someone from his office. While they were in line for dessert,

Kristen saw another familiar face coming her way. Andrew Everly and another man that she didn't recognize.

Andrew ran the newest gallery in town and when Kristen had accidentally bumped into his car, he'd suggested she work off the damage by having a show at his gallery. It had been a success, and they'd had drinks after. She liked Andrew, he was easy to talk to, but the timing hadn't been right as she still wasn't over Sean at the time. The breakup had been too recent. She'd heard recently that he'd started dating someone pretty seriously, and she was happy for him.

"Kristen, and Kate, great to see you both. I don't think you know my brother, Tyler? I talked him into moving here too and he actually just bought the cottage next to you. Meet your new neighbor."

Tyler frowned. "I haven't moved in yet. I just had a few things delivered this week, the rest is coming later this week."

Kristen held out her hand. "It's nice to meet you. Once you get settled, stop by and say hello." She couldn't help noticing how opposite they were in looks and demeanor. Andrew was all light and sunny with his blonde hair and laid back, friendly ways.

Tyler was taller than his brother by several inches and was long and lean. He radiated darkness, with almost black hair that was a bit too long and untamed, not straight or wavy but something in-between, a tousled look. His eyes were just as dark and he looked as though he'd rather be anywhere but there. She wondered what he did for work, but didn't want to ask.

"My brother is a moody artist. You might know his work, he writes the Tyler Black books," Andrew said proudly.

"The Tyler Black?" Kate sounded impressed and Kristen felt bad that she hadn't a clue who Tyler Black was.

"What kind of books do you write?" Kristen asked and a curious look flashed across his face.

"He writes international espionage blockbusters, featuring a female assassin. The books are amazing," Kate answered for him.

"Thanks. They're fun to write." A slight smile briefly appeared on Tyler's face and faded just as quickly.

"I'm sorry that I haven't read one yet. I read in spurts and when I do it's usually lighter women's fiction or romantic comedy," Kristen explained.

"Where are you moving from?" Kate asked.

"Manhattan. I still own a condo there. I might put it on the market in six months or so once I figure out if I want to live here year round. I needed a change." He didn't say more than that, but Kristen sensed that something big had happened that made him want to get away. Nantucket was a great place for that, to hunker down and soak in the fresh air and peace. She sensed that he needed to heal from something, and she hoped that he'd find whatever he was seeking.

"Well, we're on our way out. It was nice seeing you both," Andrew said and Tyler nodded in agreement. Kristen yawned. It was getting late, but she knew Sean was nowhere near ready to go yet. He was generally one of the last to leave any party they attended. She'd teased him once that he suffered from FOMO—fear of missing out, and he'd actually agreed.

"I hope you get to know your new neighbor. I'd love to talk books and writing with him sometime," Kate said as they watched them leave.

"He doesn't seem anxious for company, but maybe once he's settled in, he'll be more interested in getting to know people," Kristen said, but she had her doubts.

"I have all of his books. You can borrow one, if you want to check them out."

"I'd love that." Now that she'd met her new neighbor, she was curious to see what his books were like.

3

"Hello? This is Ruth Smith. I'm trying to reach my husband, Tom Smith. He's not answering his cell phone and I'm getting concerned. He was due home earlier this afternoon." The voice on the phone was a bit shaky.

Lisa glanced at the clock. It was just after seven, Sunday evening. And Tom Smith was the guest that had prepaid but never checked in.

"I haven't seen him," she said.

There was a long moment of silence, followed by, "But, he told me he was booked at your inn?"

"He was," Lisa confirmed. "He prepaid actually, but he never checked in. I thought that maybe he'd missed the boat and would be a day late. I'm very sorry that I don't know more than that." She paused and then gently suggested, "You may want to contact your local police as well as the Nantucket police department and local hospitals. Not to alarm you, but that's what I'd do."

"All right, I'll do that." The woman's voice was wobbly with fear and confusion and Lisa's heart went out to her. She didn't have a good feeling about it as she couldn't imagine why someone would prepay and then not show up or even call, unless something had happened that prevented him from doing so. She didn't want to scare the woman even more by saying that though.

She hung up the phone and returned to the kitchen island where Rhett and one of her best friends, Paige, were sitting with empty plates in front of them. They'd just finished Sunday dinner, Lisa's favorite, homemade meatballs and sauce. She'd invited Paige to join them as they hadn't really had a chance to catch up since Paige had returned from Florida.

She'd spent the winter there as usual, but had met someone and it got serious fast, but ended suddenly a week after she returned to Nantucket. Her new love was supposed to join her and spend the summer on Nantucket, but instead, he'd broken up by text message and stayed in Florida. Lisa had expected Paige to be heartbroken, but she'd taken it all in stride.

Lisa filled them in on the phone call and they both looked puzzled. "Telling her to call the police and hospitals was good advice. Best thing to do. If anything happened here, they'll know about it." Rhett stood and brought his plate to the sink and rinsed out his wine glass.

"No more wine for you? I was just going to top off our glasses," Lisa offered.

Rhett shook his head. "I'm going to leave you two ladies to chat. There's a new book that's calling my name."

He wandered off as Lisa put the dishes in the dishwasher and added more of the Josh Cabernet to their glasses.

"Strange about that woman's husband, isn't it?" Paige said as she lifted her glass to take a sip.

"It is. I thought it was odd when he didn't show up the first night, but the entire weekend is even stranger. I hope wherever he is, that he's okay."

"Maybe he never even made it to Nantucket? I haven't heard anything in the news. It's been a quiet weekend here."

"Speaking of quiet, how's your new neighbor?" The one woman on Nantucket that neither of them could stand, Violet Jones had moved into the house right next to Paige. Violet was…interesting. She fancied herself irresistible or something as she was always dressed to the nines in outfits designed for men to look twice—a bit too tight or too low cut, but not quite over the line to trashy. She was attractive, but there was a bitchiness about Violet at times that was hard to swallow.

She seemed to like men much more than women and regarded all women as competition. She'd been a nuisance when Lisa was trying to get her bed-and-breakfast approved by the town selectman. Violet had been one of several that had protested and managed to have the inn's approval delayed. So, Lisa didn't have any warm feelings toward the woman. Especially when after all the protesting, she moved out of Lisa's neighborhood and into Paige's. Paige had been horrified when she saw Violet walking into the house next door.

"She's a menace," Paige growled. "She plays her music so loud that I can sometimes hear it with my door closed, and she keeps the oddest hours."

"What do you mean?"

"She must be a night owl. She's up until all hours of the night and people often come to visit her at ten or eleven or even later. It's really the strangest thing."

"Hmmm, that is odd."

"Well, yeah. Especially as it's always men. Men visiting late night is odd."

"She doesn't seem to have many women friends," Lisa observed.

Paige laughed. "Well, she has plenty of men friends. If I didn't know better…"

Lisa leaned forward, intrigued. "What do you mean?"

"Well, I'm sure it's not what I'm thinking, but late night visits from multiple men does make you wonder."

Lisa's jaw dropped. "You're not suggesting...."

Paige nodded. "I know it seems far-fetched, but if you saw the daily stream of men, you'd wonder too."

"Is it always different people?"

"I'm not sure. I haven't watched that closely to be honest. I have noticed that some of the cars parked in her yard look familiar though as in I've seen them there more than once."

"Maybe she's just dating around? Keeping her options open," Lisa wondered.

"Hmmm, maybe. It probably is something like that."

"So, how are you doing? Are you over John?"

Paige laughed. "I am so over John. He was fun, but I think I knew it wasn't going to be anything long term. At my age, I'm fine with that. Especially now that I'm going through menopause. It's the strangest thing."

Lisa agreed fully. She took a sip of wine and set her glass down. "I'm still getting hot flashes, but they're not as bad as they were six months ago. Are they bad for you?"

"Not too bad. For me it's been more mental, the realization that a part of my life is over and that having kids is no longer an option. It feels like a loss, even though I'd sort of made peace with that years ago. It just never happened for me."

"I thought you didn't want kids?" Lisa asked gently. Paige had always been so independent and seemed to love her freedom.

"I don't want them now, but growing up, I assumed I'd have them. I had this vision of being married with four kids by age thirty-five." She took a sip of wine and smiled wryly. "I was way off on that. It's fine though. My brother and sister both had kids and being an aunt is pretty amazing. You get to spoil them rotten, get your kid fix and then go home."

"That's very true," Lisa agreed. But she felt for Paige. Lisa loved having her four children and when her husband had died, her kids had been there to support her. And they were all good people, whose company she enjoyed very much. She couldn't imagine not having them around. And it was why she'd decided to turn her house into a bed-and-breakfast—so she could afford to stay on Nantucket and be near her children and closest friends.

"Speaking of children, Kate and Kristen saw Chase at that charity event the other night."

Paige raised her eyebrows. "Chase? I don't think I've ever seen him dressed up. That doesn't seem like his kind of thing."

Lisa laughed. "It's not. But the rumor seems to be true. He is dating Lauren Snyder."

"Really? I see her for sale signs all over the place. For someone so young, she seems to be doing well."

"Hmmm. She does seem to be focused. Though I have to confess, it makes me a little uneasy that she's turned her attention to Chase. She's not his type."

"And you don't want to see him hurt."

Lisa nodded. "I know there's not a thing I can do about it, but I just don't have a good feeling about it. Hopefully I'm wrong."

BETH ANDERSON WAS HUMMING ALONG to the radio as she sat at her desk typing on the computer. Chase smiled at the sight of her. She looked cute with her light red hair in a ponytail and a sprinkling of freckles across her upturned nose. He knew she hated being called cute—though at barely five feet tall, Beth was resigned to it. She looked up and smiled when Chase stepped into the office. He'd been out on a job all day and had about an hour of paperwork to do, new bids mostly, before he could call it quits for the day.

Not for the first time, he was grateful that she was there. He'd be lost without Beth. She was always in a good mood and it was contagious being around her. She was one of his younger sister, Abby's, best friends and had worked for him for several years, when his business expanded to the point where he needed help full-time. Beth took all incoming calls, handled all invoicing and accounting for clients and basically ran his business as his office manager.

"Long day?" She asked as he picked up a stack of mail and couldn't stifle a yawn.

"Busy. Good though." There was no shortage of work, plenty of people looking to build new homes or renovate existing ones. "How was your day?" he asked before stepping into his office.

"Oh, it was good. It sounds like you're going to get the Green job. Ed Green called earlier and had tons of questions. He seemed to like my answers. I told him to call you directly if he had anything else, but he said he thought he was all set and would be in touch soon with a decision."

"That's great!" Chase was impressed. Beth had learned so much about his business that she was able to handle almost any question that came her way. Her smile turned to a frown though as she answered the phone and turned to him to say, "Lauren's on line one. I just put her through to your office."

"Thanks." Chase felt the same little thrill of excitement every time Lauren called. It was obvious that

Beth wasn't as keen on her, but Chase quickly forgot about that as he went into his office and shut the door behind him. He glanced at his cellphone, wondering why she hadn't called it, and saw that his ringer was off and there was a missed call from her. The red light on his desk phone was blinking, and he quickly picked up the call.

"Hey, what are you up to?" He imagined that Lauren had been running around all day, showing houses and maybe even selling one. She was a real go-getter, and he was proud of her and how well she was doing.

"I'm making dinner and hoping that you haven't eaten yet and might want to join me. There's something I want to talk to you about."

He was intrigued, wondering what she wanted to talk to him about and also by the fact that she was making dinner. He didn't know she could cook.

"Well, that's an offer I can't refuse. What time do you want me to come by?"

"How about two hours from now?"

"Perfect, I've got about an hour of paperwork and then I'll go home, jump in the shower and head over."

He hung up and whistled to himself as he opened his email and reviewed the first of several new bids he was going to be sending out. He mostly worked by referral these days and both of these new projects were from friends of people he'd built homes for. He was just finishing up when there was a soft knock on the door. He waved at Beth to come in and she opened the door a crack.

"I just wanted to say goodnight. I'm heading out."

He stared at her for a minute trying to figure out what was different and then he realized she'd taken her ponytail down. Her hair fell in a wild tangle of curls just past her shoulders. Her lips looked pinker than usual too.

"You look nice. Are you heading out somewhere?"

Beth's cheeks flushed at the unexpected compliment. She nodded. "I'm meeting a few girlfriends for after-work drinks and tacos at Millie's."

Millie's was one of Chase's favorite places. It was off the beaten track out by the beach and was hugely popular with the locals. The food was California style Mexican, light and fresh and the service was really fast.

"That sounds good. I love Millie's. Lauren is having me over for dinner, said she's cooking something."

Beth laughed. "You don't sound all that enthused. I'm sure it will be great."

"You're right, I'm sure it will be. See you tomorrow."

Chase headed home soon after Beth left. He lived in a small studio apartment over the garage of his best friend Jim's house. It was the perfect situation. Jim was happily married to his high school sweetheart and Chase had his own space and the rent was cheap, for Nantucket. It was just a place to sleep, and it gave him a chance to save as much money as possible, so that he could eventually buy and build something himself.

He picked up a bottle of Lauren's favorite chardonnay on the way to her place. She had a roommate but Tracy was in New York City for a few weeks. She did something in sales and was always flying off somewhere. Lauren said it made her the perfect roommate because she was never there but still paid half the rent. They shared a two bedroom home that Lauren bought a few years ago as part of the Covenant program on Nantucket. It was a great program that allowed year-round residents with moderate incomes to buy homes at below the current crazy market prices.

The only stipulation was that they couldn't flip them for huge profits. When they sold, it had to be to another Covenant qualified buyer. She'd timed it well as her income when she first moved home to Nantucket was much lower. It was clear that she was doing very well now. Her business had grown quickly in the few years she'd been selling real estate on Nantucket.

As he pulled onto Lauren's street, he felt the same rush of excitement that came whenever he was around her or sometimes even just when he thought about her. He had a history with Lauren, that had made him resist her this time, for as long as he could. But finally, curiosity and desire won, and he slowly began to allow himself to spend time with her and to fall for her, again. There was just something about Lauren that drew him and kept him coming back.

He never quite knew where he stood with her—she pulled him close, then pushed him back and pulled him close again. He'd been wary at first, because of how she'd treated him in high school. They'd gone on exactly one date and then she moved on to someone else, an older, more popular football star. It had crushed him at the time as she'd never looked his way again, until a few months ago, when he ran into her at the Chicken Box, a local bar. She'd grown even more beautiful since high school.

After college, Lauren worked in the real estate market in Boston for a few years and then came home to Nantucket and put everything she'd learned to good use. She and her brother ran one of the biggest real estate brokerages on the island. The only bigger one was the one run by Kristen's boyfriend, Sean. When they'd run into each other, Chase had literally bumped into her in the crowded bar and she'd spilled her full drink. He'd apologized profusely, bought her another one and one for himself and they ended up talking for several hours.

He'd noticed her immediately when she first moved

back to Nantucket, but he didn't imagine they'd have anything to talk about, so he'd steered clear. But once they actually sat down and started chatting, there was an instant connection and they'd bonded over their love for real estate.

He'd been impressed by her knowledge of the local market and of home construction in general. And she'd seemed equally impressed by how well he was doing with his building business. At the end of the evening, when she hinted that she might like to get together sometime, he didn't hesitate to suggest a time and place, and they'd been dating ever since.

He hadn't mentioned her to his family yet though, because he knew they'd be concerned, given their brief history in high school. His sisters and mother were very protective. He was closest to his youngest sister, Abby, and as it turned out, she'd been at the Chicken Box that night too and had seen him talking to Lauren.

She'd called the next day and asked him about it, but at the time it was so new that he'd simply told her the truth, that he'd bought her a drink and they'd chatted a bit. He left out the plans to go out because he didn't know if it would go anywhere. But now that Kate and Kristen had run into them at the golf club, he figured he owed Abby a call to catch her up, now that it seemed a little more serious. At least it was for him, he still wasn't as sure about Lauren. She could be hard to read at times.

But he figured it was a good sign that she'd invited him for dinner. As he pulled into her driveway, he could see her silhouette in the window and candles flickering on the dining room table. When he reached her front door, it flew open, and she pulled him in for a hug.

"I heard your truck," she said as he handed her the bottle of wine and stepped inside.

"Something smells delicious. What are we having?"

"Braised short ribs. My grandmother's recipe." There was a twinkle in her eye as she said it. It was the first time she'd mentioned even having a grandmother. Maybe she'd passed on already. Chase didn't give it another thought as Lauren led him into the kitchen where she found an opener for the wine and poured them each a glass.

"Are you hungry?" She asked as she set out a plate of cheese and crackers on the kitchen island, which had three chairs on one side. Chase took his wine and sat in one of the chairs.

"I could eat." He was actually starving and looking forward to trying Lauren's cooking. He reached for a cracker, added a slice of cheese and popped it in his mouth as he watched her pull a steaming pot out of the oven. She set it on the stove and pulled a casserole dish of mashed potatoes from the oven too.

"Let's give this a few minutes to rest and then we can dive in." Lauren picked up her wine and joined him at the island, sliding into the chair next to him. They chatted about their days for a few minutes and then Lauren made a plate for each of them and brought their dinners to the dining room table that was set with fresh flowers and two lit candles.

"Bring the wine over, would you, we could both use a topper. And a few paper napkins."

Chase did as instructed and added wine to both their glasses before sitting. He took a bite and was pleasantly surprised by how good it was. Lauren knew that Chase loved short ribs. If it was on the menu, he usually ordered it and there were several places on the island that did a great job. Lauren's was as good as any he'd had and he told her so. She seemed pleased by the compliment.

"Thank you. My grandmother used to say that if you cooked meat long enough at a low temperature, it would be well worth it."

They ate quietly for a few minutes, enjoying the food until Chase asked. "Is she still around?"

"Who?"

"Your grandmother."

"Oh! No, she died about ten years ago, at least."

"That's too bad. At least she passed on her love of cooking to you."

Lauren choked a bit on her wine and after a moment caught her breath.

"Went down the wrong way," she said.

"Are you sure you're okay?"

She took a big sip of wine and smiled brightly. "I'm fine. I do have something I want to run by you though. Something exciting, for both of us. It's work-related."

"Oh? What's that?" He was intrigued by her enthusiasm and curious about what she had in mind.

"So, you know my brother's friend, David Wentworth?"

Chase nodded. Everyone on the island and most of the East Coast knew David Wentworth, he was into everything, hotels, casinos, office-buildings. He hadn't built anything on Nantucket yet, but rumors were that he was sitting on a sizable lot of land, which only gained in value with each passing year.

"He wants to do a new development, out near Millie's restaurant by the beach."

"What kind of development?"

"He's thinking high-end condos, multi-level, all with panoramic ocean views."

"That could work." It was actually a great idea. Most of Nantucket was free-standing homes. But lots of people liked the convenience of luxury townhouses. And they could charge whatever they liked and get it.

"So what they were thinking is that you could build

them, under David's direction, and Rick and I could sell them, as the exclusive listing agents. It's a win-win for all of us!"

Chase felt a rush of excitement followed by a small twinge of warning. David Wentworth had the reputation of being difficult to work for and sometimes even stiffing his contractors. He wasn't too worried about that as Lauren knew him and Nantucket was a small place. But, still, he'd need to meet the guy and learn more about what he was proposing. It could be an amazing thing, if it actually happened. And he was grateful that Lauren had recommended him for it.

"Thank you for suggesting me. It could be an incredible opportunity, if it happens."

"Oh, it's happening. There's no doubt about that!" Lauren laughed as she stood to clear their plates. Chase followed her to the kitchen with their empty wine glasses and dirty napkins. He handed Lauren the glasses and when he put the napkins in the trash, he noticed that there were two cardboard to-go boxes with Keeper's restaurant stamped on the side, along with an empty plastic container that said 'Country Crock mashed potatoes'. So much for Grandma's special recipe. At least Lauren had good taste in takeout—he'd always loved the short ribs at Keeper's.

4

The following Tuesday night, Lisa had an impromptu family dinner. In the cold, winter months, she saw her children more often, at least once or twice a month for Sunday dinner, but in the summer months everyone was just so busy that it was usually last minute whenever they happened to be available.

Rhett was away for a few days, checking on his restaurants in Manhattan and while Lisa enjoyed her alone time, she felt like seeing her kids and mothering them a little. Even though they didn't need much these days. She could still feed them. And so she did, and splurged on something they all loved, lobster rolls and homemade clam chowder. She'd spent the afternoon making the chowder, and the kitchen smelled heavenly

—of bacon and butter, potatoes and onions, cream and of course, fresh local clams.

Abby and Chase were the first two to arrive. Chase picked Abby up along the way. He'd always been protective of his baby sister, especially now that Abby was pregnant. Jeff wasn't able to join them. Abby had explained that he already had plans with a few friends. Chase helped himself to a bottle of beer, while Abby poured a glass of iced tea and added so much sugar to it that Lisa and Chase exchanged glances. Abby saw it and laughed.

"I don't do this all the time, so don't worry. Just now and then, when I feel like treating myself. Yes, I know too much sugar isn't good, but it's better for me than the fake stuff." Abby had quit Sweet 'N Low cold turkey when she found out she was pregnant and it was one of the hardest things for her to give up

"No one is judging, honey," Lisa said as she poured herself a small glass of red wine and settled on one of the chairs around the island. Everything was ready. The lobster rolls were in the refrigerator and the chowder was keeping warm on the stove. A few minutes later, Kate and Jack arrived and Kristen was right behind them.

"Sean couldn't make it?" Lisa asked. She'd told Kristen that he was welcome, though secretly she'd hoped that he was busy. She wasn't overly fond of the man, though she was trying to be open-minded and to give him a chance, to see what Kristen liked about him. But it was still a mystery to her.

"I didn't ask him," Kristen said simply. Kate looked like she was going to comment, but then instead walked over to the chowder and lifted the lid and breathed deeply.

"Yum! This smells amazing."

Lisa laughed. "Well go ahead and help yourself. The bowls are on the counter and I'll put the lobster rolls out."

Once everyone helped themselves, they brought their food to the big dining room table and took a seat. They all raved about the food, which warmed Lisa's heart and she had to admit, the chowder had turned out unusually good. She'd added a pinch of thyme, which added a subtle hint of flavor.

"So tell me all about the event at the club. Did you have a good time?" Lisa looked at Kristen and Kate when she asked the question.

"It was much better since Kate and Jack were there," Kristen said.

"We weren't the only ones there," Kate said as she glanced Chase's way. He looked uncomfortable for a moment, but then said, "Yeah, I was there too. It was kind of a last minute kind of thing. A friend had tickets. It was fun, actually. Food was great."

Lisa had already heard that Chase was there with Lauren. Nantucket was a small place and even though neither Kristen nor Kate had said a word, two of Lisa's friends had called the next day and mentioned that they'd seen Lauren with Chase and didn't they look so cute together? She smiled at her son.

"Really? A friend? Anyone I know?"

Chase hesitated for a moment before saying, "Lauren Snyder. I ran into her a month or so ago and we've been spending some time together."

"I see her real estate signs everywhere lately. She's a busy girl." And she didn't seem Chase's type at all, but she could see that he was smitten. She remembered he'd had a crush on her in high school too and how that had ended. He'd sworn that it hadn't bothered him a bit when she dumped him for someone else, but Lisa knew it had hurt. She hoped that he was treading carefully.

"She is. She's doing great. And it's not a done deal yet, but she recommended me for a huge development project that David Wentworth is doing here on the island."

"David Wentworth? Really? Are you sure that's a good idea? I'm not sure I'd want to work with him. He has a reputation of being…difficult," Kate said.

"I know. I thought about that, but he knows Lauren

and her brother, so I think it will be fine. They're handling the sales for the project."

"Well, I think it sounds like a fantastic opportunity," Abby said and he looked at her gratefully. Abby always supported him, no matter what.

"It does sound exciting." Lisa chose her words carefully. "Even if you decide not to do this project, you're still doing wonderfully, Chase. We're all proud of you."

"Of course we are," Kate agreed.

Kristen smiled and gave his shoulder a squeeze. "They'll be lucky to have you, if you do it."

After they finished eating and all the dishes were done, they went outside to the big farmer's porch that overlooked the ocean, and relaxed in the comfy outdoor chairs for a bit.

"How are sales this week?" Lisa asked Kate. She was referring to her mystery novel which had done better than any of them had expected. Kate was hard at work on the next book in the series and Lisa was eager to read it.

"They're still pretty good! I'm actually meeting Philippe tomorrow for lunch and he's going to share some marketing tips, a few new things he's tried recently, to give me ideas on how to keep the sales going.

"Oh, that's nice. Is he still dating that very young model? I saw him a week or so ago when I was out to lunch with Sue and he was coming into the restaurant as we were leaving, but he was by himself."

Kate laughed. "He's moved on several times since he dated her. I'm not sure Philippe will ever settle down."

"He needs to find someone closer to his age," Lisa said.

"Do you want me to tell him that?" Kate asked and Lisa shook her head.

"No, of course not. It's really none of my business. He just seems like a nice boy. I hope he finds someone soon."

"I'm sure he's not worried about it. He's been traveling a lot lately. He's off to L.A. at the end of the week for two months, to shoot a new mini-series for Netflix."

"How exciting! Is anyone ready for dessert yet? I have skinny cow ice cream sandwiches in the freezer," Lisa told them.

Abby jumped up. "I'm getting one. Anyone else?"

"I'll take one," Chase said.

Everyone else shook their head. Lisa was stuffed, she almost never saved room for dessert. She knew Abby and her ice-cream cravings though. She'd gotten her favorite flavor, mint with chocolate.

Once she returned with their ice cream, Lisa remembered something she'd wanted to tell them.

"So, remember how that I had that prepaid guest that never checked in?"

"I hope you didn't refund him?" Kate said.

"I haven't. Not yet. I still might though. Anyway, he never showed up at all."

"He didn't come the next day? I figured he just missed the boat," Kate said.

"No, but his wife called looking for him. It turned out that he did go somewhere for the weekend, but it wasn't here. And when she called, early Sunday evening, he hadn't come home yet."

"Have you heard anything since?" Kristen asked.

"Well, I suggested that she call the local police and hospitals and that was the last that I expected I'd hear of it. But you know Sue volunteers at the hospital?" She glanced around the porch and explained that she helped out every Tuesday by wheeling patients from their room to get x-rays or MRI's. "So, anyway, she goes into this one room to pick up a middle-aged man for an x-ray and about fell over when she checked the name of the patient and realized it was the same as the fellow that was supposed to stay here. Tom Smith.

"So his wife must have found him then if she called the hospital?" Kristen said.

"But what was he doing in the hospital? And where did he go if he never checked in here?" Kate asked.

"I wondered the same thing," Lisa said, then added, "Not that it's really any of our business."

KATE MET Philippe for lunch downtown at the Club Car restaurant at noon the next day. She was a few minutes early, and he was ten minutes late which was normal for both of them. He came rushing in and found her already seated and checking messages on her phone. She jumped up and gave him a hug. He pulled her in tight and smelled of leather and salt. He slid his jacket off and sat across the table from her.

"I'm so sorry I was late. I was down at the pier getting some great shots. The light was perfect."

"I didn't know you were into photography?" Philippe was good at just about everything, so she imagined his pictures would be impressive too.

He grinned. "It's a new hobby. I'm teaching myself Photoshop and wanted to have some good shots to practice with."

"I'm hopeless with Photoshop. Graphics and I don't get along. How are you? I'm glad I got to see you before you head out to the west coast again."

"It looks like I'll be there closer to three months. I was hoping for two, but it may take longer as one of the actors I wanted isn't available as quickly as the others.

But we're going to make it work. I got everything I asked for this time. It's going to be good." Philippe's expression reminded Kate of the Cheshire Cat. He was very pleased with himself. As he should be.

He was in the enviable position now of being able to call the shots almost totally. He'd previously explained to Kate that as show runner, he was in charge of the story vision and oversaw everything right down to asking for the talent he wanted and approving all casting decisions. And his last project had gone so well, that he was a golden child.

"I'm so happy for you. Are you still working on the new book too?" Philippe had made a name for himself as a top selling mystery author before one of his books was made into a film and another into a series on Netflix.

"Done, I shipped it off to my editor last Tuesday. I'll have edits to make, but I can mostly focus on this new project now."

Kate admired his productivity and wished she had even a fraction of his confidence.

Their server came and took their drink and sand-wich orders. They both ordered turkey clubs.

"But enough about me. What about you? Your book is still doing awesome. I checked the ranking this morning. How's the new one coming along?"

Kate bit her lower lip. She'd been expecting the

question. She dreaded it now when her family asked, and especially Jack, who asked often, but she hoped that Philippe might be able to help.

"It's not. I think I'm suffering from a bad case of writer's block. I haven't written a new word in two weeks. I don't know what's wrong with me, but nothing is coming, and I'm getting nervous. My preorder deadline is looming."

Philippe nodded. "Second book syndrome. Perfectly normal." He looked up as their server returned and set down two tall glasses of iced tea. He squeezed a lemon into his and took a sip, then looked her in the eye.

"You're afraid to fail. Don't be. Just have faith that the words will come and they will be good. Even if they don't seem it at first. They can be fixed."

"I know. That all makes perfect sense. But they just aren't coming at all. I open up the word doc and stare at the blank page. It's alarming."

"Here's what you do. Jot down everything you know about the story. Then either take a drive or jump in the shower. Both work the same for me to shake things loose. It will bring the ideas and you'll know what to do."

Kate took a deep breath. "Okay, I'll try it."

"Good. Now, what else is new? How are things with you and Jack? Are you engaged yet? Baby on the way?"

"What? You are too much. No to both. Jack's great though. We've only been living together for a few weeks, but it's going well. Maybe a little too well." The thought had crossed her mind more than once lately. That it was too easy with Jack.

"How could it be going 'too well'?"

"Well, we've never had any kind of a disagreement. It's just all too easy. None of my other relationships have been like this, though some started out this way. I guess I'm just worried about when the shoe is going to drop. I've honestly never been this happy in a relation- ship before and I'm not used to it," she admitted.

"Well, I'm certainly no relationship expert. But something tells me that's how it's supposed to be, easy. People always talk about relationships being work, but maybe that isn't necessarily true. Maybe when you find the right person, you don't have to work so hard."

"I hope you're right."

"I hope so too, and I wouldn't mind finding that kind of a relationship myself. It sounds pretty special."

A few minutes later, their sandwiches were deliv- ered, and they caught up on other island gossip as they ate. For a writer that mostly worked alone in his huge waterfront home, Philippe seemed to know just about everyone and was up on all the juicy gossip. He kept Kate entertained for over an hour, through coffee and a dessert that they shared. It was a daily special, homemade blueberry crumble and Philippe talked Kate into helping him eat it. She only managed a few bites though. When they finished, he insisted on paying and she finally accepted on the condition that she and Jack have him over for dinner when he was back on the island.

"I'll make my mother's famous lobster quiche. Jack loves it."

"I can't wait. Be sure to tell him I said hello." He and Jack were poker buddies and even though Philippe and Kate had briefly dated, they'd really never been more than friends as Philippe reminded Kate a little too much of her ex-fiance, Dylan, a photographer who she'd found in bed with one of his beautiful young models.

Like Dylan, Philippe was also impossibly handsome and admittedly not in any hurry to settle down. So, as a boyfriend, he was not a good choice, but as a friend, he was pretty special. He'd encouraged Kate to finish her book and had introduced her to some of the people he knew at Netflix, which had led to an option on her book.

"I will. And have fun in L.A."

"Always do. Oh, I'll nudge Kurt and Kelly, see if they can get things moving on your option."

"Thanks, Philippe. Safe travels."

5

Paige Henry stopped at Bradford's, the local liquor store, on the way home from the grocery store. She hadn't done a major shop since she'd been back from Florida and she was out of just about everything, including wine. She wasn't much of a cook, so she was looking forward to settling in for the night, maybe heating up one of the pre-made meals she'd just bought and sitting on her porch with a glass of wine and her latest romance novel.

She wanted to keep busy, to get her mind off how empty the house felt. She'd never really minded living alone, but John had been practically living with her in Florida—he was over almost every night, and even though she didn't miss him all that much, she'd gotten used to the company, just having another presence in the house.

"Hey, Paige, good to see you. Did you stay longer in Florida this year? I haven't seen you around in a while?" Peter Bradford, the owner of the shop, asked as he rang up her two bottles of cabernet. She'd known Peter for almost as long as she could remember. He was a nice guy, a year or two older than her and like Lisa, he'd lost a loved one to cancer-Julie, his wife of over 20 years. It was a second marriage, but it had been a happy one and she knew this past year must have been brutal for him. Julie had died less than nine months after being diagnosed.

"I did. I just got back last week. How've you been?"

"I'm hanging in there. It's been hard, but it's true what they say. Once a year passes, it does seem to get a little easier. It's been almost a year and a half now."

"Cancer sucks," Paige said impulsively and immediately regretted the outburst. But Peter laughed.

"That it does. But I have a new roommate and that seems to be helping. Lily keeps me on my toes." Peter looked happy and Paige mentally whipped through her people catalog and came up empty. She didn't know anyone on Nantucket named Lily.

"I don't think I know her. Is she new to Nantucket?"

Peter chuckled. "You could say that. Let me show you a picture of her. She's really a beauty."

"Ok." Paige thought it was a little odd that he

wanted to show her a picture of his new girlfriend or roommate, but whatever.

He flipped through his phone until he found the picture he wanted and then turned it so Paige could see. She immediately laughed so hard that she brought tears to her eyes. The picture was of a tiny, adorable, orange kitten.

"I can see why you've fallen so fast. She's a cutie."

"She's a good girl. I wish I had half her energy." He turned the phone back and flipped to another picture to show Paige. "I don't know if you'd have any interest or if you know of anyone looking to adopt a kitten, but Lily's brother, Bailey is available. He's the last of the bunch of kittens that my next-door neighbor is trying to get rid of. I'm half-thinking of getting him myself, but I didn't want to take on too much too soon."

Paige took one look at Bailey's little orange face, his long skinny tail and what looked like crossed-eyes and felt something shift inside.

"Where do I go to get him?" Maybe she could pick Bailey up on the way home, because there was no doubt, Bailey was moving in with her. She'd always had a cat or two, but after her most recent one, Betty, died after nearly twenty-one years, she'd needed a longer grieving period.

Peter jotted a phone number on a business card and handed it to her.

"If you give her a call now, she might be there. She's usually around most afternoons."

Paige took the card and slipped it in her pocket. As soon as she was in her car, she pulled it out and called the number. An older woman answered and was thrilled when Paige asked about Bailey.

"He's here waiting for you. Come by anytime. I'm not going anywhere today."

Paige decided to go home first and brought all her groceries inside and put everything away before heading back out to Mrs. Crosby's house. She had second thoughts for a slight moment as she walked toward the front door. Until she saw Bailey and picked him up and the little cat burrowed into her neck and purred so loudly that it made her laugh.

"He likes you! He's not usually that friendly."

"Can I take him now?" Paige didn't want to go home without him.

"Of course you can. He hasn't had his shots yet, but he's just eight weeks old as of yesterday, so you can bring him into your vet and get it taken care of anytime.

"Great, I'll do that." Paige had brought Betty's old carrier with her and lined it with clean towels right out of the dryer, so Bailey wouldn't be confused by smelling another cat. He bounded into the carrier and immediately chased his tail while Paige fastened the doors. He meowed frantically all the way home, but it was a short drive and ten minutes later, they were inside and she opened the carrier doors to let him out. He spent the next hour exploring every nook and cranny of the house until he was so exhausted that he flopped down on the sofa and fell fast asleep. Paige ran out while he was sleeping and bought everything else she'd need, a litter box and litter, and plenty of cat food.

When she returned and was getting everything out of the car, her new neighbor Violet, was outside getting the mail. She waved when she saw her and then to Paige's dismay, she walked over to talk to her.

"Paige, right? I know I've seen you around before."

"I think I last saw you at the town meeting when you and a few others spoke up against my good friend Lisa's new bed-and-breakfast."

Violet hesitated for a moment, then smiled brightly and said, "Well, that turned out all right in the end, didn't it? She has her license now."

"She does, yes. Can I help you with something?" Paige was anxious to get inside and check on Bailey.

"Oh no. I just wanted to say hello, since we're neighbors now. If you ever need anything, just holler."

Paige couldn't imagine what she'd ever need from Violet, but she nodded anyway.

"Sure. I'll do that." She took a step toward the house and Violet did too.

"Do you have a cat?"

"I do now, just got him today, so I need to get this stuff in before he does something he shouldn't."

"Oh! How exciting, well I won't keep you then."

"Goodbye, Violet."

"I MISSED YOU." Rhett took the last sip of his coffee and waited for Lisa's reaction before getting up for a refill. They were sitting in the dining room at a little past eight in the morning and no one else was up yet. He'd arrived home late the night before, coming in on the last flight over and hadn't wanted to wake her. They'd chatted about nothing in particular for the past twenty minutes as he sipped his first cup of coffee and Lisa ate a toasted bagel, and then out of nowhere, Rhett said that he missed her. Lisa's heart swelled because she'd missed him too, more than she'd expected.

"I missed you too. It was quiet around here with you gone," she admitted.

The lazy smile that she'd grown to love spread across his face as he reached out and took her hand.

"I've grown to really like it here. I don't have any plans to leave again anytime soon."

Lisa matched his smile with one of her own. Rhett

was telling her in his own way, not to worry about him leaving. And it had been in the back of her mind and was keeping her from opening herself up fully to him. Just in case this was a temporary thing. She knew he had other business interests off-island and there were many business owners that closed up shop after Columbus Day weekend in October and went elsewhere for the winter. She didn't want Rhett to go elsewhere.

"I'd like to stick around through the winter, if you'll have me." He gave her hand a gentle squeeze and met her eyes with his own, waiting.

She simply nodded and said, "Yes. Yes, of course I'll have you. I've gotten kind of used to having you around."

He chuckled and let go of her hand. "Good, because you're stuck with me, now." He got up and refilled his coffee and helped himself to a blueberry muffin.

As he sat back down, there was a knock at the front door, surprising them both.

"Were you expecting anyone?"

"No. Certainly not this early. I'll go see who it is." Lisa got up and made her way to the front door. She glanced out the small side windowpane and was surprised to see Brad Livingston there. He'd been on the football team with Chase and after graduating from college he'd joined the Nantucket police force. He smiled awkwardly when Lisa opened the door to let him in.

"Nice to see you, Mrs. Hodges. I'm sorry not to call first, but I was just down the street when I got word to talk to you, so I figured I'd stop by and see if you might be available."

"Of course, come on in, Brad. How's your mother and your dad? I hope they're well?" Lisa hadn't seen them in ages, now that the kids were grown.

He nodded. "They are, thanks." He shifted back and forth and Lisa could tell he wasn't entirely comfortable with whatever it was he needed to talk to her about.

"Have a seat, Brad. Can I get you a cup of coffee or tea?" He sat carefully on one end of her living room sofa. She chose a single chair facing him and waited to see what his visit was all about.

"No, thanks. I'm good. This shouldn't take too long hopefully. I just have a few quick questions."

"All right. How can I help?"

"Well, does the name Tom Smith ring a bell?"

Lisa nodded. "Yes, he was supposed to check in last Friday."

"And you never saw him?"

"No. And the strangest thing was he prepaid for the weekend too."

"He never showed up, but he paid in full? That is strange. Was it supposed to just be him or was there anyone else coming with him?"

"The reservation was just for one person. But I did get a call from his wife on Sunday. He was due home in the early afternoon and she never heard from him. I told her to call the local police and hospitals, both here and at home."

"She did call us. We had to give her some bad news, unfortunately. Someone drove him to the ER and dropped him off. He was having chest pains. They ran some tests and were prepping to fly him to Boston, but he didn't make it."

"Oh, that's awful. But why are you investigating? Was there something else going on?"

"We're not sure. It's certainly strange that he paid in full to stay here for the weekend and never showed up. He didn't come into the hospital until Sunday and we don't know how he got there or where he was all weekend. He wouldn't say, which the nurses made a note of. They thought it seemed strange."

"I wish I could help, but I'm afraid I never saw him at all."

Brad nodded and stood up. "I figured as much, but we have to check everything. There's not much to go on."

"Do you think he was murdered? You said it was a heart attack?"

"It was probably natural causes, but given the situation, we owe it to his wife to see what we can find out. Heart attacks can be induced you know."

"Oh. I never thought about that." Lisa didn't know such a thing was possible.

"It's unlikely, as I said, but at least we can give his wife peace of mind by letting her know for sure and maybe getting some answers for her as to where he was. Though, maybe that's information she won't want to know. Hard to say."

"Good luck, Brad. I hope you figure it out. I wish I could have been more helpful."

"You have been. Enjoy the rest of your day."

6

Kristen wiped a stray piece of hair off her forehead and tried to tuck it back into her ponytail. She'd been outside all afternoon, working on a landscape scene that focused on the gorgeous Virginia roses that lined her back yard. They were the prettiest deep shade of pink and she'd been meaning to paint them ever since she moved into her cottage a few years ago. Her place was small, but it was perfect for her. She used the dining room as her art studio and spent most of her time in the warmer months, on the enclosed porch.

She stood to stretch and loosen up muscles that were tight from sitting for too long. She needed to be better about taking breaks to walk around, but when she was in the zone, those good intentions flew out the window. She assessed her work for the day and was relatively pleased with what she saw. It wasn't done yet, but it was coming along nicely and she might be able to finish up the next day, as long as the light was right.

She turned at the sound of a large truck coming down her quiet street. It looked like a moving truck and stopped at the cottage next door. She hadn't seen any signs of her grumpy new neighbor yet, but guessed he'd be making an appearance soon.

Sure enough, a moment later, a black BMW sedan pulled up behind the moving truck and she watched as Tyler got out of the car and walked up to the truck. She couldn't hear anything, but a moment later, the back door of the truck opened and three movers started moving furniture into the house. Tyler disappeared inside and Kristen watched the activity for a few minutes, as the movers carried in heavy-looking dark wood furniture, a desk, leather sofas, all very masculine looking, from what she could see. Much of it was wrapped in moving blankets, so she could only catch an occasional glimpse. She didn't expect to see much more than that as Tyler didn't strike her as interested in having her over for tea anytime soon.

She smiled at the thought and stood to put her supplies away for the day. Then went inside to take a hot shower. Once she was dried off and finished combing out her hair, she went to call Sean to confirm what time they were meeting for dinner. It was their three year anniversary and when he'd suggested dinner out, she'd assumed it was to celebrate the milestone. Though they went out to dinner regularly.

She had a missed call and a voicemail from Sean and clicked play to listen.

"Hey, Kristen, I need to reschedule. Something has come up at work, a new client is in town that I need to meet with. I'll call you tomorrow."

She sighed. There was no mention of their anniversary. She was pretty sure it was just going to be another dinner out in Sean's eyes so not a big deal to him to cancel. They could do it another night. For Kristen though, it was the push she needed to do what she'd been putting off.

She had the whole night ahead of her and no plans and she was in the mindset to do something. She didn't want to bother Kate as she knew she likely had plans with Jack now that they were living together. But maybe Abby might feel like doing something.

She dialed her sister and Abby picked up on the first ring. And as it turned out, she had no plans.

"I'd love the company. I'm not really up for going out, but maybe we can get some takeout and relax here. Jeff's out for the evening."

"Great, I'll see you around six then. What can I bring?"

"Well, if it's not too much trouble, I am running

low on Ben and Jerry's Cherry Garcia. That's my favorite flavor this week."

Kristen laughed. "I can do that. See you in a bit."

She stopped at Stop and Shop for Abby's ice cream and then at Bradford's Liquors for a bottle of chardonnay. When she arrived at Abby's, she handed her the brown bag.

"Here you go. Ice cream for you, and wine for me." She took the wine into the kitchen to find an opener and her sister followed and got a wine glass out of a cupboard for her. Abby raised her eyebrows when she saw the label on the bottle.

"La Crema, nice. That used to be my special occasion wine. Jeff would get it for my birthday or our anniversary." She stopped and looked at Kristen intently.

"Today's not a special occasion, is it?"

Kristen filled her wine glass to the rim and put the bottle in the refrigerator to keep cool.

"It was. It's our third year anniversary, and we had dinner plans."

"Uh-oh. I think I know where this is going."

Kristen nodded. "Same place it always goes. Sean totally forgot. I think our dinner plans were just another night out to him. That's all we really do is go out to dinner, not that I usually mind, but still."

"He canceled?"

"Yeah. He's meeting with a new client. I wouldn't mind so much if it wasn't such a common thing, and I actually thought that maybe since he'd made dinner plans, that he had something special in mind for our anniversary. That was silly of me."

"No, it's not silly. Let's go into the living room and get comfortable. Are you hungry?"

Kristen hadn't thought about food all day and realized that she'd missed lunch again. Her stomach rumbled at the mention of food.

"I guess I am."

"Let's order Chinese. It will take a while, but they deliver." Abby found the menu and called in an order for chicken fingers, lo mein, egg rolls and house fried rice. Kristen thought it was too much food, but Abby couldn't decide so they just ordered everything she was craving.

Kristen sank into Abby's plush living room sofa and felt like she was being wrapped in a big hug.

"Isn't that sofa great? You can see why it's hard to get out of it. I've been living on it lately." Abby was sprawled across the matching love seat, sipping an iced tea.

"I don't want to get up either. How's Jeff? You mentioned that he's out tonight?" Abby seemed content lately and Kristen was glad that they'd seemed to have ironed out their issues.

"He's good. We're good." Abby patted her stomach and smiled. "I've been the one falling asleep early lately, so I've been encouraging him to go out more with his friends. I'm in nesting mode, content to just curl up on the sofa and click."

"That sounds nice. Are you watching anything good? I need a new show to follow."

"I have two new favorites. An older Lifetime show, Drop Dead Diva, it's super cute and Killing Eve." She laughed. "They're like night and day, but both are good."

"I'll check them out." Kristen noticed that her sister was still absentmindedly patting her belly.

"How's everything going with the baby? How are you feeling?"

"Good! The morning sickness is pretty much gone and now I'm just hungry all the time. And it's not like I needed any help there. I do have some news though....it's a bit of an update about the baby."

"You're not having a boy?" Kristen guessed.

Abby laughed. "Yes. It's a girl. They thought it was a boy on the first ultrasound but turned out to just be a shadow. I guess that happens a lot. They have a better picture now."

"A girl. How awesome. Of course it would be just as exciting if it was a boy."

"I was secretly hoping for a girl, though I'd love a

boy too. I just think it's going to be so much fun buying little girl outfits."

Kristen smiled. "There's no shortage of those on the island. Congratulations!"

"Thank you. I just found out today, so you're the first to know."

Kristen was glad to hear it. "Well that's one bright light on an otherwise darkish day."

They chatted for another half-hour until there was a knock on the door and their takeout arrived. Abby got paper plates, napkins and utensils while Kristen set the boxes on the coffee table and opened up the cartons. They were both too comfortable to leave the living room sofas.

Once they filled their plates, they ate their fill. After Abby had moved on to her ice cream, and Kristen added a splash more wine to her glass, Abby asked the question that Kristen had been thinking about ever since Sean's call.

"So, what are you going to do about Sean?"

Kristen took a slow sip of wine and sighed. "I think it's time. I gave him a second chance, against my better judgment. Nothing has really changed. And I've realized this isn't the person I want to spend the rest of my life with."

Abby nodded and Kristen knew she understood.

"You need to be happy. So when will you let him know?"

"Soon. Very soon."

TWO DAYS LATER, after ignoring several voice messages, Kristen called Sean. He was apologetic, especially in his third voice message when he apparently remembered that it had been their anniversary. She wasn't moved by his messages though. She was over it and clear about what she needed to do. But she didn't want to do it over the phone.

So, she texted him and said she needed to talk to him and asked if he was free for lunch. He didn't reply right away, and when he did, his message didn't surprise her. They never went to lunch, not during a work day. So, he likely suspected what was coming.

"I can't do lunch. I'm booked solid all day. But I want to see you. Can we meet for dinner? How about Millie's at six?"

Kristen really didn't want to do a long, drawn out dinner. But Millie's was her favorite restaurant, and the service was so fast, that it would be over and done with quickly.

"Fine, see you at six."

WHEN KRISTEN PULLED into the parking lot at Millie's, she saw Sean's Mercedes parked out front. He was probably in the bar upstairs, that's where he liked to sit whenever they came here. The ocean views from the second floor were spectacular. Kristen made her way upstairs, glad that he hadn't suggested the Straight Wharf or one of the other fancier places downtown that would have been more his typical choice. She liked the food at Millie's, but she also liked the beachy, casual feel of it, with the light wood, open space and lots of windows.

Sean was seated in the bar area at a high top table for two. Every seat at the bar, and all the surrounding tables were full. They were lucky that they didn't have to wait. Sean stood when she reached the table and pulled her in for a kiss, but she turned her head slightly so the kiss landed on her cheek.

"Thanks for agreeing to do dinner instead of lunch. Today was too crazy."

Kristen just nodded and pulled her sweater around her a bit tighter. It was warm out, but the air conditioning was on full force and it was chilly.

"What do you feel like having? We could get a bottle of champagne?" Sean suggested.

"I'm not in the mood for champagne." She definitely wanted a drink though. It would help her to get through this dinner. She was dreading the conversation and Sean wasn't making it easy for her. He'd worn the navy blue button-down shirt that she'd given him for his birthday. The color drew attention to his icy blue eyes, and he was smiling, which brought out the deep dimples on both sides of his mouth. He hadn't colored his hair yet, and even the slight dusting of silver was attractive on him.

Their server, a young man who looked sixteen but was probably in his early twenties, came by to take their drinks order. They both ordered margaritas and when he returned with their cocktails, they put their food order in, fish tacos for both of them and some guacamole and chips to share. Less than two minutes later, he returned with the appetizer, and Kristen was grateful for the speed of the place. She opened her mouth to begin the dreaded conversation but Sean beat her to it.

"Let's eat first and save the talk for when we finish. Let's just enjoy our dinner, can we do that?" He flashed his most persuasive smile as he picked up a chip.

Kristen nodded. She wanted to get it over with, but it would be easier to wait until after they ate. Dinner would be even more awkward otherwise. She dipped a chip into the buttery smooth, homemade guacamole and glanced toward the bar. Two familiar faces caught her eye. Tyler and Andrew were sitting at the bar, sharing a plate of nachos. Neither one of them saw her, and she brought her attention back to the table where Sean was going on about his latest whale client and the biggest ever real estate deal he was working on. Kristen was happy for him, but she didn't really care to hear all the boring details.

Fortunately, their tacos came out a few minutes later and Sean stopped talking to eat. Once they were done, and their plates were cleared, he glanced toward the kitchen as if he was waiting for something and Kristen began to have a sinking feeling in her stomach, which grew when four servers came toward the table, clapping and singing, "Happy Anniversary to you!" Their server was in the lead and was holding a slice of chocolate cake with a lit candle. He set it down in the middle of the table and then they vanished back to the kitchen.

"You really shouldn't have done that," Kristen said. She knew Sean was trying his best to head off the conversation she'd been planning. He was hoping she'd forgive like she always did. But she wasn't going to this time.

"Of course I should have. You're important to me. I actually have something much better than cake for you." He looked quite pleased with himself as he reached into his pocket and pulled out a small velvet box. And then he stood and came over to her side of the table and got down on one knee.

Kristen felt lightheaded and a bit horrified. Had he misread things that much? Or was he just so confident that he thought he could manipulate the situation the way he wanted? He opened the box and Kristen gasped. It was a ridiculously big diamond ring. Huge. It was the type of ring that people stopped and stared at. Showy and no doubt insanely expensive and it just emphasized how little Sean knew her. It was a beautiful ring, but it wasn't something she'd ever pick out herself. She couldn't imagine wearing it.

"Will you marry me?" There was no declaration of love, just the question. But he did seem sincere and it put Kristen in a very awkward position. The whole bar was watching—including Andrew and Tyler. If she said no, she'd be publicly embarrassing Sean. She couldn't do that to him, no matter how badly she wanted to.

"What do you think? Do you love it?" Sean took the ring out of the box and slid it onto her ring finger, not even waiting for her response.

"It's beautiful."

He took that as a yes, stood and pulled her in for an enthusiastic kiss. Everyone around them cheered, while Kristen felt a mix of anger and sadness. A year ago, she would have been excited, thrilled even at the thought of getting engaged to Sean. It was a long time coming, but finally she realized that she deserved better. She'd been in love with the idea of Sean, but when she really looked more closely at their relationship, at the way he spoke to her sometimes and at what was most important to him, well, it wasn't her. And she didn't want to spend the rest of her life with someone who didn't always make her feel good about herself. Truth be told, she didn't want to spend five more minutes with him.

"Let's get out of here," he said as he threw a pile of money onto the table and led her out of the restaurant. When they reached his car, he stopped and took her hand. "So, back to my place? Or to yours?"

Kristen sighed. She let go of his hand and slowly slid the ring off her finger and held it out to him.

"What are you doing? Don't you want this? Us? I thought it's what you always wanted."

"I did at one point. I don't anymore. Besides, you're technically still married. Your divorce isn't even final yet."

"But I filed. Like you asked me to. And it will be soon. The ring looks beautiful on you."

Kristen looked into his eyes and gently said, "Sean, I came here to break up with you. You never gave me a chance to even have the conversation."

"But you said yes! I sensed that you were upset, and I thought this would make you feel better."

"It's too late for that. It's just not right with us, and

it hasn't been for a while. At least it's not working for me. And I don't think either of us is going to change."

"Why did you say yes then?"

"I didn't, actually. You never gave me a chance to say anything. I also didn't want to embarrass you. It was just easier to have this conversation outside."

"Huh. Well, I do appreciate that. You know, plenty of women would love that ring. You sure you won't change your mind?"

Kristen shook her head. "I'm not going to change my mind. I'm glad for the time we had together though."

Sean just stared at her, speechless. She guessed that he was more used to being the one doing the dumping. When it finally sunk in, anger followed, which she understood. She didn't expect him to be happy about her decision.

"You're making a big mistake." His voice was tight, his eyes stormy.

She took a deep breath and politely said, "Goodnight, Sean. Thank you for dinner."

7

Beth's text message came as Chase was leaving the work site to head back to his office for a meeting with David Wentworth, the developer Lauren referred him to. They were meeting at two and it was only twenty of. Chase would be at his office in less than five minutes, which he'd thought would be plenty early enough.

"He's here already! What should I do with him?"

Chase thought for a moment. His office was nothing fancy. It didn't have a reception area because Chase typically went to his clients and met them at their homes or home sites.

"Send him into my office and please see if he wants a coffee or anything. I'm on my way and will see him shortly."

"Great, I'll let him know."

Chase walked into his office a few minutes later and Beth made a face as soon as she saw him. It was clear she was not a fan of David Wentworth.

"I offered him coffee and he asked for a cappuccino, can you imagine? He's in your office. Have fun!"

Chase took a deep breath and entered his office. David Wentworth was sitting behind Chase's desk, as if it was his own and was busy typing on his phone. He looked up when he saw Chase.

"Ah, there you are. Sorry, I know I was a little early. Do you want your chair back? Hope you don't mind that I made myself comfortable?"

Chase did mind. He thought it was quite rude, but wasn't about to say so. He didn't want to start things off on the wrong foot. So, he smiled and held out his hand.

"Good to see you again. No, of course I don't mind. I'll just sit here." He sat in one of the two leather chairs across from his desk and it was an odd feeling, as if he was in David's office. And David immediately took charge of the meeting.

"So, Lauren says good things about you. I did some asking around and heard more good things. This could be a very big opportunity for you. Very big." David smiled as he leaned back and put one of his feet up on the desk and his arms behind his head. He looked relaxed and powerful and his belly huge. It was big and round and Chase had to stop himself from staring at it. His designer suit fit perfectly though and his thinning hair was combed over to make it appear fuller. His complexion was ruddy, his eyes hooded. There were rumors that he was a big drinker and it appeared true with the telltale flush of his skin. He did everything to excess it seemed, but so far, he'd been extremely successful.

"Yes, I'm grateful for the chance," Chase said. He'd also done his research on the man sitting at his desk and learned that he had a huge ego that required regular stroking. Chase could play the game if he had to. Whether it would be worth it, remained to be seen. He needed to know more about what David Wentworth had in mind.

"So, let me tell you what we're doing." David spent the next half hour telling Chase all about the new project and how it was going to be a career making opportunity for him. The exposure would be tremendous. Tremendous! He tended to repeat himself often for emphasis and was quite a salesman. Chase thought it was interesting that he was trying to sell him so hard on what seemed like a no-brainer. Any builder would jump at this opportunity, wouldn't they?

And then David Wentworth casually mentioned the budget he was proposing for the project and Chase's alarm bells began to ring. It immediately sounded low and after he did a few quick mental calculations, he realized it was even lower than he'd first thought. His profit margin would be dangerously thin and didn't leave much room for unexpected expenses or delays which almost always happened.

"So, what do you think? Are you on board? I can have my girl write up a contract and get it over to you later today. We're ready to move on this."

"The project sounds wonderful," Chase began. And it did, the condos as described would be lovely and David wanted all high end quality materials and finishes. But he didn't seem willing to pay for them. "Is your budget flexible? Materials tend to cost a bit more on the island and then there are always things that come up."

But David shook his head. "Nope, no flexibility I'm afraid. We put a lot of research into this and know where we need to be for costs." He looked Chase in the eyes, smiled and said, "I know your profit margins might be a bit lower than you're used to, but the tradeoff could be huge. You'll make it up in volume and exposure."

And the alarms grew louder. Chase wasn't willing to trade all of his profits for added exposure. Especially on an island where everyone for the most part already knew him, and he was plenty busy as it was. But still, he decided to play the game for a bit.

"It's certainly tempting. If you want to have her send over the contracts with your specs, I'll dig into this a bit more and get a better sense of what my exact costs will be. And then I can let you know."

David stood and held out his hand. "Fair enough. You do that. And then sign and get the contract back ASAP. Ideally today. As I said we're ready to rock-and-roll on this. If you're not in, I need to get someone else ASAP."

"I can get back to you by tomorrow." That would have to be good enough. Chase needed to really think this through.

"Tomorrow it is."

Chase walked him out and as soon as the door was closed, Beth told him what she thought of David Wentworth.

"Please tell me you're not going to do business with that man? I have a horrible feeling about him. He was flirting with me and it grossed me out. As if I'd ever go out with someone like him. He's older than my father!" She looked thoroughly disgusted at the thought and Chase didn't blame her. David Wentworth also had a reputation of being a womanizer and especially loved being seen with women half his age.

"I'm sorry about that. I'm not sure what I'm going to do, but it doesn't look good, based on the numbers he was tossing around in our meeting. He's going to send over a contract with more specifics and I'll see if it makes sense for us."

"That's if he pays you at all. I did some digging around on the internet and there are a lot of unhappy contractors that have worked with him. I'd hate to see that happen to you."

A few hours later, the contract came over with the budget and all the approved costs broken out. Chase went through it carefully more than once and the numbers just didn't add up. If the slightest thing went wrong, he could actually lose money on the project. The only way he could make money would be by using lower quality materials, which was suggested in the contract. Everything that was visible would be the advertised quality, but the wood below could be a lesser grade.

Chase knew that plenty of builders were willing to do that, to cut costs on things that didn't show to the homeowner, but that wasn't how he worked. His homes were built to last. After reading through the contract fully, it was an easy decision. He was out. He'd tell David in the morning though so that it seemed as though he put more thought into it and really considered the offer. He didn't want to insult him by saying no too quickly, especially when Lauren was involved in introducing the two of them. He dreaded telling her more than David, actually. She'd been so excited about this for him.

CHASE'S PHONE rang as he was about to bite into the Italian sub he'd picked up for dinner on his way home. He was sitting at his small kitchen table with the sub and a bag of chips. He could see from the caller ID that it was Lauren. He thought about letting the call go to his voicemail and calling her back after he ate, but he hated putting things off. Better to get it over with.

"Hey Lauren. How was your day?"

"Insanely busy, as usual. What about you? How did your meeting go with David Wentworth? I'm so excited that you're going to do this with us. It's going to be so great."

There was a long, uncomfortable moment of silence before Chase spoke. "We met and he sent over his contract. The numbers just don't work for me, Lauren. There's not enough profit and if one thing goes wrong, it could actually wind up costing me money."

"Did you already tell him no?" Was Lauren's first question.

"No. I told him I'd get back to him tomorrow, but I'm not going to do it."

"You'd be crazy to give up this opportunity. It could be so huge for you!"

"Not if it costs me money. Exposure is overrated when everyone already knows who you are."

There was another long, awkward pause before Lauren said, "Can't you find a way to cut costs somehow? Use less expensive materials for all the stuff that doesn't really matter?"

Chase didn't like what he was hearing. "Do you mean use an inferior quality on the underlying materials, the part people can't see?"

"Yes, exactly that! Builders do that all the time."

"That's what David suggested too, but it's not how I work, Lauren."

"Don't you want to be successful and grow your business? This could help you get to the next level." She was right, it definitely would. But at what cost?

"That's not how I roll. I can't promise one thing and then deliver something else, something less than the buyer expects."

"But, it's okay by David! Everyone does it."

"Not me. I'm sorry, Lauren. I do appreciate you

suggesting me for the project. I wish I was able to do it, but David says there's no flexibility on the budget."

"Well, that is disappointing. He'll probably give it to one of your competitors."

"He probably will. I don't doubt that."

"Okay, well I have to go. I'm running late to meet Tracy."

"No problem. Are we still on for Thursday night? I was thinking maybe the Straight Wharf for dinner. We haven't gone there yet."

More silence. "I don't think I can do Thursday. Something has come up. I'll let you know about a different day."

"Let's pick it now, Friday works or Saturday, your choice."

"I'm not sure. I'll have to get back to you. Good bye, Chase." She seemed suddenly anxious to end the call.

"Bye, Lauren. Call me once you figure out your schedule," he said. But she'd already ended the call.

PAIGE WAS STARTING to worry about Bailey. The kitten was nowhere to be found. He'd been running around earlier and following her from room to room like he usually did before she ran out to run some errands. She'd been back home for an hour and was surprised when he hadn't come rushing to the door to greet her like he always did.

She was madly in love with him and the feeling seemed to be mutual. Although he was a terror and was into everything, just a nonstop ball of energy that always wanted to play, but when he tired out, he always wanted to snuggle with Paige. His favorite spot was the crook of her neck and he'd burrow there while she was lounging on the sofa or in bed, and just purr. It was adorable, but after a while also annoying, especially when she was in bed, trying to sleep. He purred so loudly, that she finally tried picking him up and putting him out in the living room and closing her bedroom door, but that didn't work. He'd sit outside the door and howl until she let him back in and then he'd burrow happily against her again and eventually they'd both drift off to sleep.

So, it wasn't like him to ignore her. She'd been walking all around the house calling his name and looking in all his favorite sleeping spots. He was an indoor cat, so she knew he was in the house some-where. She was just making herself a cup of tea when there was a knock on the door and her jaw dropped when she looked out the window and saw Violet standing there holding Bailey.

She flew to the door and opened it. "He was outside? How on earth?"

Violet stepped inside and handed Paige the kitten. Bailey snuggled against her. She petted his small head and rubbed off a bit of dirt. It looked like he had been rolling in it.

"Did you go anywhere this morning? He must have slipped out," Violet said.

"I did, and my arms were full with dry-cleaning I was dropping off. He must have run between my legs. I'll have to be more careful. He's fast."

"I saw him rolling around in the mulch and had a feeling he wasn't supposed to be there. He's a friendly little guy, came right over when I called his name."

"Thank you. Would you like a cup of tea? I was just going to make myself one." The least she could do was offer her something since the woman brought back her cat.

"Sure, I'd love that."

Paige made two cups of hot water and added herbal tea bags to both. She set them on the kitchen island, her favorite spot. The island was v-shaped with chairs along the side and the stove was in the center, so whoever was cooking could face their guests and have a nice ocean view at the same time.

"This is a stunning kitchen. You must love to cook," Violet said.

Paige laughed. "I should, but I can barely boil water. I don't have the patience for cooking, but I'm excellent at heating things up."

Violet smiled. "I'm the same way. Never learned to cook or had any interest in it. I make a great sandwich though and prefer to go out to eat or do takeout. It's easier, especially since it's just me."

Paige discovered as they chatted for the next half-hour that Violet really wasn't so bad. It turned out they had other things in common too. Neither one had married and both enjoyed being social and going out often. Paige was still a bit annoyed that Violet had been so against Lisa's bed-and-breakfast being approved and finally asked why she'd voted that way.

"To be honest, I didn't really care one way or the other as it didn't affect me. But Lillian Hardy was all up in arms and I sort of owed her a favor. She asked me to speak up against it, so I did. I am glad it got approved eventually though. How is it doing? Is she making a go of it?"

"She is. Lisa is doing a great job. I'm really proud of her. I don't think she would have been able to stay here otherwise. Nantucket is so expensive."

"It really is. How do you manage? Do you still work?" The question was a bit nosy, but Paige didn't mind.

"I make a little money selling stuff on eBay.

Collectibles mostly, like Hummel figurines. I pick them up cheap at yard sales and they get good prices sometimes. But I'm also fortunate that I was an only child, and when my parents passed about ten years ago, I came into a little bit of money. Enough that I was able to leave my full-time job on the Cape and move here. This house was where we vacationed. My parents bought it many years ago."

"That's great. It's been a bit of a struggle for me, to be honest. I was lucky that this rental house was part of the Covenant program. I'd been waiting for something to come available."

"That's a wonderful program. I'm glad it worked out for you. What do you do for work?" Violet didn't seem to go anywhere during the day other than an occasional trip to run errands, so Paige guessed she must do some kind of work at home.

"A little of this, a little of that. I've tried selling some stuff on eBay too, but I don't seem to have the knack for it." She glanced at her phone as a text message beeped through. "Oh, I need to run. I just realized the time. A friend is on his way over. I have a favor to ask if you don't mind?"

"Sure, what do you need?"

"I'm going away for a long weekend and am waiting on a package to be delivered. It's a box of lemon swirl cheesecakes, so it's perishable. If I give you a key would you mind keeping an eye out and bringing them in and putting them right into the refrigerator?"

Paige laughed. "Only if I can have a bite of one of them sometime. Of course, I'd be happy to."

"Great, I'll drop a key off before I head out. I'm leaving Friday and will be back sometime Tuesday afternoon."

"Are you going anywhere exciting?"

"New York City. Meeting up with some college friends for a special birthday celebration."

"Oh that sounds fun. Thanks again for bringing Bailey by. I really appreciate it."

"Of course. That's what neighbors are for."

8

K risten felt a mix of emotions after finally ending it with Sean. It was like a huge weight had been lifted, relief was the main thing, but there was a significant amount of sadness too. She realized she was grieving the death of their relationship and the best way for her to do that was to dive into her work. She let her emotions bleed onto the canvas and surprised herself by the depth and beauty of the two paintings she produced in the days following the breakup.

She hadn't heard from Sean at all, which wasn't surprising. He'd been furious but also seemed to realize that she was serious and it was over. She suspected he'd rebound quickly and get back out there. But she wasn't in any hurry herself. She was content to hunker down for a while, spend time with her sisters and friends and when it felt right, maybe she'd dip her toe in the dating pool again. But at the moment, it wasn't appealing in the least.

When she was done working for the day, she was utterly exhausted as the hours had flown by. She wasn't going anywhere, so she hadn't bothered to shower and had already decided that her dinner was going to be a big bowl of Ben and Jerry's Caramel Almond Brittle ice cream. It was made with almond milk and was her favorite flavor. She didn't indulge as often as Abby, but she did treat herself to an ice cream dinner now and then.

It was a gorgeous night, warm with a soft breeze, and the sun had just set as Kristen took her ice cream out to her screened-in porch and curled up on her sofa. She was just about done when she jumped at the sound of a knock on the porch door. She looked up and saw Tyler standing there. She hadn't even heard him walk up as she was facing the opposite way and was watching the evening news.

"I'm sorry, I didn't mean to startle you. I just wondered if you might possibly have a flashlight I could borrow? I have one but it's still packed away somewhere and I think I blew a fuse."

"Sure, come on in. I know I have one here somewhere."

Tyler stepped inside and glanced at her almost empty bowl of ice cream.

"That looks good. What is it?"

"Dinner." She grinned and knew he meant what flavor. "Caramel Almond Brittle. Want some?"

"Maybe another time. I have a steak on the grill."

Kristen went into the kitchen and to the cupboard where she kept lightbulbs and flashlights. She found a big one, made sure it worked and handed it to him.

"Here you go. Do you need a hand? I think the cottage layout is probably identical to mine, so it could save time if I show you where the fuse box is."

"Sure, if you don't mind. That would be great."

She followed him across the yard to his cottage. It was already getting dark out and when he opened the door to the basement, it was pitch black below. Tyler shined the light down the stairs and this time Kristen went first and sure enough, the fuse box was in the same spot as hers. He fiddled with the switches and a moment later, the power came back on.

"What were you doing that caused the power to short out?" She wondered.

"I had too many things plugged into an extension cord strip in my office. I knew I was pushing my luck but was being lazy. I'll have to figure something else out."

They made their way back upstairs and Tyler

handed her the flashlight and raised his eyebrows when he noticed her bare ring finger.

"Where's your sparkler? Andrew and I got a good look at it from the bar. You did well for yourself. I suppose congratulations are in order?" He teased and Kristen was glad to see he had a lighter side. He was much friendlier than the last time she saw him.

"I gave it back to him. I'd actually been planning to break up with him when he surprised me with the ring."

Tyler whistled softly. "That must have been awkward."

"It wasn't ideal."

"You didn't say no though? It looked like you were celebrating."

"I didn't want to embarrass him in public. I waited until we were outside."

"That was decent of you. He probably thought there wasn't a chance you'd say no."

"He's not a bad guy. We had some good times, but ultimately, we just want different things."

"Yeah? What do you want?"

"Just to be happy. I'm not into the showy stuff, I don't care about any of it. And I'm not looking to jump into anything anytime soon. I need a break to just be by myself for a while. I was alone all day today and it was wonderful."

Tyler nodded. "I'm the same way. When I'm deep into writing a book, I sometimes don't leave the house for days and lose all track of time. Then eventually I get out and do something social, but if it's a party like that country club thing Andrew dragged me to, I can only take it for so long. It's too much peopling and it's draining. I need to be alone to recharge."

Kristen understood completely as it pretty much described how she felt. She much preferred small get-togethers to huge gatherings.

"Your brother is the complete opposite. He's a social butterfly."

Tyler laughed. "He is. I think he introduced me to half of Nantucket in one night. He knew everyone there and he feeds off that energy."

Kristen glanced around the room. The layout was about the same as hers, but the overall look was very different, with all dark woods and black leather. It looked like he was mostly finished unpacking except for a few boxes by the kitchen.

"Looks like you're settling in quickly."

"I'm just about done. I should finish the rest tomorrow. Then I can get back to work."

"What are you working on now?"

"A new suspense thriller. I just finished the outline a few days ago, and I'm eager to dive in."

The smell of something delicious suddenly tickled

her nose and Kristen realized she was keeping him from his dinner.

"I should let you go. I bet your steak is almost ready. If you need the flashlight again, come by anytime."

"I will, thanks again."

As they walked toward the door, Kristen noticed the few remaining boxes had the name of a local beer on them, Second Wind Brewery, in Plymouth.

"That's my favorite beer. Looks like you're a fan too?"

Tyler looked confused for a moment then followed her gaze to the boxes and shook his head. "I just got those from a liquor store to use for packing. I don't drink. Or to be more specific, I don't drink anymore. I've been sober for three years now."

"Oh, congratulations. I didn't know." She felt a bit awkward, unsure of what to say.

"No reason you would have known. It's all good."

"Okay, have a good night then."

THE ONE THING Lisa didn't love about running a bed-and-breakfast was the cleaning. She didn't mind tidying up and making the beds as much as she hated chasing stray hairs around the tub. But it was a necessary evil. Every dollar counted and even though the guests paid the cleaning fee, if she hired it out, she'd be losing that money. She was sorely tempted at times though. Especially today as she was stiffer than usual and exhausted by the time she finished taking care of all five rooms. Her feet had been bothering her lately, mostly when she first got out of bed, but now her knees were achy too and she wasn't sure what, if anything, she could do about it. She'd been so tired lately too. She knew she was overdue for her yearly physical, which she'd been planning to skip, but maybe she should just go and see if there was something that might help.

As she made her way downstairs, she heard her phone ringing and picked up her pace. She answered it just in time.

"You sound breathless. Were you out running? Or maybe I've interrupted something. Is Rhett with you?" Paige fired the questions off and Lisa laughed.

"None of the above. Rhett is at the restaurant and I was upstairs cleaning."

"You should hire someone to help you with that, even if it's just a few days a week, to give you a break."

"That has crossed my mind more than once lately. It's something I'm definitely considering even if it's part-time."

"So, do you have plans tonight?"

"No, I'm totally free. Rhett is working late and I was just going to catch up on some reading."

"Good, want to come over for a girl's night, just you, me and Sue? We haven't all gotten together since I got back. Everyone's been so busy."

"I could do that. What time and what can I bring?"

"Let's say about six-thirty and just grab a bottle of your favorite wine along the way. I always like whatever you pick out."

"Are you cooking?" If so it would be a first.

"What do you think? Of course not, but I do great takeout. I was thinking Pad thai, spring rolls and duck curry from Thai House."

"Sounds good. I'll bring something white then."

A few hours later, after showering and changing into her oldest, most comfortable jeans and her favorite soft pink sweatshirt, Lisa headed out. She stopped at Bradford's liquors on the way and stood staring at the white wine section trying to decide what to get. Peter Bradford, the store owner, wandered over once his customer paid.

"Hey Lisa. How've you been? Can I help you find something?"

She smiled. "I'm open to suggestions. I told Paige I'd bring wine. She's having my friend Sue and I over for dinner."

"Do you know what you're having?"

"Thai, so might be a little spicy."

"I like a lively Sauvignon Blanc from New Zealand, like Monkey Bay, with spicy food. Paige likes that one too, she buys it now and then."

Lisa was impressed that he remembered what kind of wine Paige liked.

"That's perfect then. I'll take a bottle." He rang her up and she was on her way. As she turned onto Paige's street, she saw Sue's car pulling into the driveway. Lisa parked next to her and they walked in together. Paige opened the wine and poured a glass for each of them while Sue set a bakery box on the counter.

"What's that?" Paige asked.

"Mrs. Harvey's brownies." Mrs. Harvey owned a tiny bakery in Beach Plum Cove and she made the fudgiest brownies.

"Oh, you shouldn't have. I'm never going to get rid of these ten pounds," Paige protested and then added, "But of course I'm glad you did."

Paige handed them each a glass of wine, and Lisa almost dropped hers when something furry ran across her foot. She looked down and saw Bailey, the kitten Paige had told her about. She set her wine down and scooped him up. He purred loudly and then wriggled frantically for her to put him down. She did and he ran over to Paige, who automatically picked him up and he snuggled into her.

"He's adorable."

"He is, isn't he? He's a handful, into everything, but he's so cute I can't get mad at him." She put Bailey down and raised her glass in a toast.

"Cheers!"

Lisa laughed and lightly tapped her glass against the others. "What are we toasting?" She asked as Paige set a plate of cheese and crackers on the island counter top and then joined Lisa and Sue who were already seated.

"Oh, I don't know. Just glad to be back on the island and finally catching up with my two best friends." She reached for a slice of cheese and then added, "Our food should be here in about a half hour." She took a sip of her wine and then reached for the bottle and laughed when she noticed the label.

"This is one of my favorites. How did you know?"

"I got it at Bradford's. Peter told me you like it."

Paige looked pleased to hear it. "He's a great guy. So tragic what happened to Julie." They were all quiet for a moment and then Paige said, "Speaking of tragic, have you heard anything more on that guest that had the heart attack? Sue, you actually met him?"

"I did. He didn't seem too bad when I saw him. They had stabilized him and were running lots of tests and taking X-rays. I guess the results weren't good because they were going to med-flight him to Boston, but he had a second heart attack and didn't make it."

Paige reached for another cracker. "And Lisa, you said the police came by asking you questions? Odd that he never checked in. What do the police think?"

"I haven't heard anything. I think they are just asking questions because his wife was so distraught that he never came home and had told her he was going to be elsewhere. I refunded his money. Didn't feel right to keep it given the circumstances."

"Where do you think he went?" Sue asked.

"I do have a theory about that. You saw him at the hospital on Sunday, right? Lisa asked.

Sue nodded. "Yes, Sunday morning, around ten."

"So, he was somewhere else on Nantucket. The only reason I can think of that he wouldn't have checked in would be if he had another place to stay. Maybe he was having an affair and booked the room as a cover?"

"Hmm, that's a possibility. A good one, I'd say. We'll probably never know for sure though."

"No, probably not," Lisa agreed. They changed the subject and for the next twenty minutes or so exchanged the latest gossip on all the people they knew.

When the doorbell rang, Paige jumped up to get the door and their food. It was still light out and when Paige opened the door, Lisa saw a police car in the driveway next door. When Paige brought their food over, she commented on it too.

"Violet has a visitor. First time I've seen a police car there. And we all know Brad Livingston is young, even for her, so it's not a social visit. Wonder what they want with her?" She handed each of them paper plates and they helped themselves.

"Is she still driving you crazy?" Lisa asked as she picked up a spring roll.

"No, not really. She's actually not too bad. We've chatted a few times now and she was nice enough to bring Bailey back when he snuck out one afternoon. She even gave me a key to her house."

"She did?"

"She is going away for a long weekend and is having cheesecakes delivered and she asked me to bring them in and put them in the refrigerator."

"What does she do for work?" Lisa realized she knew very little about Violet.

"I'm not really sure. She was kind of vague about it," Paige said.

"There are rumors," Sue said before taking another bite of her taco.

"I've heard them too, but I'm not sure I believe them," Lisa said.

"I haven't heard anything. I'm so out of the loop when I go to Florida. Give me the scoop."

"Well, I don't know that any of it is even remotely true," Sue said. "But there has been some whispering that Violet runs a high level escort business."

"On Nantucket? She's a madam? Has people working for her?" Paige was surprised. It didn't fit what she'd seen of her.

"No, nothing that organized. Just that she has certain arrangements with wealthy men that like to visit Nantucket." Sue added a splash more wine to all of their glasses. "I only just recently heard that. Supposedly it's why she moved to a new neighborhood. Because people were asking questions."

"Hmm, well that would fit her hours and the late night visits," Paige said.

"If it's true. It's probably just gossip." Lisa lifted her glass and paused before taking a sip. "It does make you wonder though, why the police want to talk to her."

9

"Ed Green called. He said to tell you he put a check in the mail today for his deposit and wanted to confirm that you'll be starting on his project two weeks from today. And Mrs. Harvey wants you to install an awning. I told her you'd give her a call tomorrow morning."

"That's it? No other messages?" Chase asked. A look flashed across Beth's face, a fleeting hint of pity that made him cringe. Her face was an open book and he could tell that she felt bad for him and knew he was hoping for a message from Lauren. He hadn't heard from Lauren for several days now, since he told her he wasn't going to do the condo project with David Wentworth.

"No, that's it. How was your day?" Beth's smiling

face usually cheered him up but not today. But it wasn't her fault he was in a bad mood. He took a deep breath.

"It was good, busy. I'm going to go finish up a few things." He walked toward his office, then turned back to face Beth. "It's been a busy week, why don't you pop smoke, and I'll see you tomorrow."

Beth yawned. "I'd love to if you're sure?" It had been a busy week. Chase had a dozen or so guys that worked for him and had several projects going at any given time and this week, he'd hired two more men and added another project to the mix. He knew that she'd been on the phone more than usual fielding questions and handling as much as possible so Chase wouldn't have to be bothered.

"I'm sure. Go ahead and head out."

"Thanks, Chase. You should do the same, don't work too late."

"I won't be long." Chase went into his office and shut the door behind him. He'd suggested that Beth 'pop smoke' the expression his father used to quit early because she was a hard worker and deserved it but also because he felt like being alone in the office.

He finished his paperwork and picked up his phone to call in a pizza order when it buzzed and the caller ID showed Lauren's number. It brought a relieved smile to his face.

"Hey stranger!"

"Chase, I'm soooo sorry. I meant to call you back sooner. It's just been so crazy around here."

"I thought you might be mad that I didn't agree to do the Wentworth deal?"

There was a moment of silence and then Lauren laughed a little. "Don't be silly. I do think it would have been a great opportunity for you, but it's your choice."

Chase relaxed a bit. "Good, I'm glad to hear that. What are you up to tonight? Do you want to share a pizza? I was just about to order one."

"Oh that sounds good, but I can't tonight. I told Tracy I'd do something with her. We might go see a movie and maybe grab a bite to eat. But I did want to see if you want to come with me to a wine tasting dinner at the Wauwinet Friday night? There's a group of us going, my brother and a few of his friends and Tracy might join us with her new boyfriend. It should be a lot of fun."

"Sure. I love wine tasting." He'd actually never been to one, but he liked wine well enough, and since Lauren was inviting him, he was happy to go.

"How fancy is the dress?" Wauwinet was one of the nicest and most expensive hotels on the island.

"Wear the suit you wore to the country club event, it'll be perfect. See, you're already getting your money's worth from it."

Chase laughed. He didn't expect to wear the suit

again so soon, but Lauren was right. It was a good investment and it fit him well. He was just happy for the chance to see her again. He knew he was falling too hard, too fast and should be more cautious, but he couldn't help the way he felt.

"I look forward to it. See you on Friday."

BETH LEFT the office and made her way downtown to Main Street and Murry's, the closest thing Nantucket had to a department store. She was in the mood to window shop and wasn't in a hurry to go home to the empty cottage she shared with her best friend, Jill. Jill was an ER nurse at the Nantucket hospital and worked long shifts. Beth figured she'd take her time, maybe buy a new pair of shoes and get some takeout on the way home. She didn't expect to run into anyone and laughed when she literally bumped into Abby as she came around a corner holding a stack of baby clothes.

"Hey! What are you doing here? I was actually going to call you and see if you felt like getting together soon," Abby said.

"Chase told me to head out early soon after he came in. I think he just wanted to be alone. Last I heard, he was still waiting to hear from Lauren."

Abby frowned. "She has some kind of weird power over him. I don't trust her. I never have. But he won't listen."

"He hasn't talked to her since he told David Wentworth he wouldn't do the condo project."

"Hmmm, well maybe that's a blessing in disguise if she ends things before he gets in too deep. I think it would be easier now rather than later when he's even more emotionally involved. How shallow of her though, if that's why she's not calling him."

"I know. I agree. He looked so sad earlier." It made Beth dislike Lauren even more. If she didn't want to date Chase, she should just tell him and let him be miserable and move on.

"Do you want to grab a coffee now? I was just on my way to the register," Abby asked.

"Sure. I wasn't after anything in particular. I'd rather visit with you."

Once Abby paid, they walked the short distance to India Street and The Bean, which was their favorite place for coffee and sandwiches. They both ordered a cappuccino and brought them to a small wooden table with a view of people walking by outside.

"How are you feeling?" Beth asked. She and Abby had been best friends since elementary school and she was thrilled that she was finally pregnant. They'd had a hard time and ironically it wasn't until after a failed

UVF round when they decided to wait before trying again, that she suddenly found herself expecting.

"Pretty good. I've only gained about twelve pounds so far. I thought it would have been more because I feel like I'm hungry all the time and I've never eaten so much ice cream before."

"You're not showing at all yet," Beth said. Abby didn't look even remotely pregnant.

"I'm hiding it well. The doctor said I should really pop out in another month or so."

"How are things going with Jeff?" Beth knew her friend had struggled a bit in her relationship before she finally got pregnant.

Abby smiled and leaned back in her chair. "Things honestly have never been better. Jeff is really excited about the baby and he has cut his hours back at work. Now instead of falling asleep on the couch by seven, he hangs out with me and has ice cream."

"That sounds fun."

"It's a relief. I really was half-expecting him to fall back into his old habits, working late every night and crashing early right after dinner. We've actually had a few date nights lately."

"I'm so happy for you. Jeff's a good guy. I'm glad you were able to work things out."

"Me too. But enough about me, what about you?

Have you had any dates lately? Did you try that dating app I told you about?"

Beth shook her head. "Not yet. I downloaded it to my phone though."

Abby laughed. "Well that's a step in the right direction. You really should try it out though. I know a few people who have found great guys from it."

"On Nantucket?" Beth was a little skeptical. She felt like she knew all the eligible men on the island and there was only one that interested her, and he was taken at the moment and off-limits, anyway.

"Yes, on Nantucket!"

"Maybe I'll take a closer look. No promises though."

"I just want you to find someone great. It won't happen unless you take action."

Beth laughed. "That's easy for you to say, you're happily married."

"Well, yes, I am now. But, I wouldn't be if I hadn't taken the initiative and asked Jeff out."

"You did? Why don't I remember that?"

"Maybe because it was so long ago, but yeah I was crushing on him hard. It was my sophomore year and we had the same chemistry class. I was sitting next to him, so the teacher paired us up for a project and when I finally got my nerve up, I asked if he wanted to come

over to my house to study together. We've been inseparable ever since."

"I wish it was that easy now." Beth knew she really
should make more of an effort. It had been several
years since she'd dated anyone seriously. It was easier to
just put off doing anything about it. But time went by
quickly and the sitting back and doing nothing strategy,
hoping that the person she was interested in would
eventually notice her, wasn't working out so well.

Abby smiled. "It can be that easy. You can practically order up any kind of guy you want through the
Internet or one of those apps. I think it sounds fun and
it puts you in control. I would totally do it if I was
single."

Beth knew that she would too. Abby was fearless in
many ways. Beth had always been the more reserved
one. "Maybe I will give it a try. Can't hurt right?"

10

His name was Ben and they were meeting Friday night after work at Millie's Restaurant. He seemed nice enough, but then the notorious serial killer Ted Bundy had been downright charming and handsome too. When Beth called Abby to tell her about the date, Abby was thrilled but also advised caution.

"Meet him there, don't tell him your last name and text me as soon as you get home."

Beth was happy to agree. She was equally excited and dreading the date at the same time. She and Ben had messaged on the app for about an hour the night before, and he suggested meeting the following night. So, the plan was to meet at Millie's and see how it went. She wouldn't have time to go home and change before meeting him, so she had to pick out something she could wear all day. She finally settled on her favorite dark jeans and a soft navy top that brought out the highlights in her reddish blonde hair.

She didn't usually wear much if any makeup during the day, since she was mostly by herself, but today she applied mascara, a bit of eyeliner, a dusting of rosy blush and a swipe of peachy pink lipstick. She wondered if Chase would notice. He almost never commented on her appearance other than the other night when she'd taken her hair out of the ponytail. He'd looked so puzzled trying to figure out what was different about her. It had almost made her laugh.

Beth arrived at the office a few minutes before nine. Chase sometimes came by in the morning before heading out to his worksite, but he'd stopped by the day before to get the plans for the new project, so she didn't expect that he'd be in until end of day.

As predicted, there was no sign of Chase until a few minutes past four. He was preoccupied as he walked in, busy talking on the phone. He waved at Beth as he walked into his office and shut his door behind him.

Beth stood to leave for the day at a few minutes past five, just as Chase walked out of his office. He stopped short when he saw her. She'd put on a fresh coat of lipstick and fluffed her hair.

"You look great." He grinned. "Do you have a hot date tonight?"

She knew he was teasing and decided to have a little fun back.

"I do actually. It's a first date, so wish me luck!" She smiled big and almost laughed at the surprised expression on Chase's face. She supposed she couldn't blame him though. In the nearly three years that she'd worked for him, Beth had never mentioned dating at all.

"Oh, good luck. Who's the lucky guy? Wonder if I know him."

"Ben Andrews. You probably don't know him. He's new to Nantucket."

"Name doesn't sound familiar. How did you meet him? How old is he?"

Beth laughed a little at the rapid-fire questions. "Through a dating app your sister showed me. She's been pushing me to get out there more."

Chase frowned. "Abby's never been out there. How does she know it's safe?"

Beth appreciated his concern. "I had the same worry, but Abby insisted that everyone does it now and as long as you're careful it's fine, and a good way to meet people."

"Where are you meeting him?"

"Millie's and I'm taking my own car."

Chase nodded. "Good. That's smart. I have to run too. I have to go home and put on my monkey suit again. Lauren invited me to some wine dinner at the

Wauwinet tonight." He made a face and Beth laughed. That was definitely out of his element. And no wonder Chase was in a good mood again, now that Lauren was back.

"You'll have fun, I bet. That place is gorgeous. It reminds me of the Great Gatsby with the sweeping lawns, and elegance. Almost feels like another era."

"It's not really my speed, but at least the food and the company should be good," Chase said with a grin. "See you on Monday."

BETH PULLED into the parking lot of Millie's and sat in her car for five minutes before going in. Her nerves had kicked into high gear and she seriously considered texting Ben and telling him something had come up and she couldn't make it. But then they'd probably reschedule and she'd be going through the same back and forth again. She figured it was best to get it over with. But she didn't want to arrive before he did. At a few minutes before six, she watched as a clean-cut guy about her age walked into Millie's alone. It might be him. She was too far away to tell for sure and the picture on the app was a little blurry.

He'd said he was about 5' 10", but the only single guy she saw at the bar that also had brown hair and a blue jacket was 5' 7" or maybe 5' 8" at best. But it had to be him. She plastered a smile on her face and took a step in his direction. As soon as he noticed her, he waved and smiled in return. He might not be as tall as he'd said, but he had a nice smile and plenty of hair. He was thirty-one, the same as her.

"Beth?" He asked when she reached him.

"Ben?" He nodded and held out his hand. "Nice to meet you. I saved you a seat." He pulled the tall chair back so she could slide in and sit. So, he was polite. That was a point in his favor. Once they were both seated, the bartender came over and they both ordered house margaritas, on the rocks with salt.

"So what brought you to Nantucket?" Beth asked once the bartender returned with their drinks. She took a sip and enjoyed the sweet and salty taste. First dates always reminded her of job interviews. You wanted to be yourself, but put your best foot forward at the same time. It was hard to relax. As it turned out though, Ben was pretty easy to talk to, which was a relief.

"I have a biology background and work with the Mass Audubon society as their Wildlife Sanctuary Director. It was an opportunity I couldn't pass up. What do you do?"

"Wow. Nothing as exciting as that. I'm an office manager for a construction company. My best friend's brother is the owner."

"You enjoy the work?" Ben asked as he reached for his drink.

"I do actually. I like talking to all of Chase's clients and helping him to grow his business."

They spent the next hour getting to know each other. Beth learned that Ben's favorite color was green and that he could eat just about anything except for hard-boiled eggs. The conversation was going well enough that they each ordered another drink and decided to take a look at the menu. Beth wasn't hungry enough to order a full meal and when Ben suggested they share a plate of loaded nachos, it sounded perfect.

Their conversation was light and Beth definitely felt like Ben was someone she could be friends with. But could she envision anything more than that? When their hands accidentally brushed as they both reached for the same tortilla chip, there was no spark, nothing at all. But he was really nice. So, when the bill came and he insisted on paying and asked if she'd like to go out again sometime, she said yes. Maybe an attraction would grow?

She knew that there were plenty of couples that weren't initially attracted to each other. Ben seemed interested enough, maybe in time, she would get there too. As she drove home, she wondered how Chase liked the Wauwinet and she smiled at the thought of him there in his suit. She couldn't help but remember the few times Chase's hand had brushed against hers, as she handed him a check to sign or he gave her a letter to mail, and how electric it had felt to her. And not for the first time, she wondered how it was possible for her to feel so much for someone and to have such a strong physical reaction and for him to seemingly feel nothing at all?

CHASE WAS glad he didn't have to wear a suit every day. And he wasn't even wearing an actual suit, just the blazer with dress pants and a polo shirt. Even though it fit perfectly, he still felt constricted by the formal wear. But he put it out of his mind when he saw Lauren in her blue dress. It was a shade of blue that was so light it was almost white and when she turned around, well, the back of her dress seemed to be missing and all he saw was smooth, tanned skin. It rendered him speechless.

She didn't seem to notice though and chatted non-stop as he drove them to the Wauwinet. They were meeting her roommate Tracy there with her new boyfriend and a few others. When they arrived, he saw who the other two were— her brother, Rick, and David Wentworth. He shot Lauren a questioning glance, wondering why she hadn't mentioned that those two were joining them. But she just took his arm and smiled sweetly.

"Isn't this place beautiful? They're serving hors d'oeuvres and apéritif wines out front." She led their group out front where the views of the ocean were breathtaking. Even though Chase had been born and brought up on Nantucket, he was still often in awe of the island and the ocean's beauty. There was a small crowd of elegantly dressed people there already, sipping wine and enjoying the beautiful night.

"This is the 2018, Rosa Lee Chardonnay, enjoy!" A server came by with a tray of wines and they each took one.

Lauren explained that the winery partnering with Topper's, the restaurant at the Wauwinet, was ZD Wines, a Napa Valley winery. Chase had never heard of it, but he wasn't as up on wine as his sisters and mother were. He was really more of a beer drinker, but he didn't mind wine.

As soon as the wines were delivered, another server came by with skewers of shrimp in some kind of a green sauce. Chase and Lauren each took one and Chase waited until Lauren took a bite to ask her what the sauce was.

"It's pesto and it's delicious. Try it."

He did and it was. More servers floated by with other strange looking but tasty things. A foie gras pate on toast, which Chase thought was really good until Lauren told him what foie gras was. His favorite was the spinach and cheese wrapped in phyllo. Rick and David Wentworth were off chatting and Chase forgot they were there as he and Lauren laughed and watched a family of vacationers play croquet on the lawn.

"That looks fun. Have you ever played croquet?" Lauren said.

"Can't say that I have. It does look fun." He took a sip of wine and smiled, thinking of what Beth said earlier. "Beth was right. She said this place reminded her of The Great Gatsby."

Lauren laughed. "It is a bit Gatsbyesque. Aren't you glad you came?"

"I'm glad you invited me. I was surprised to see your brother and David though. You didn't mention they would be here."

"Didn't I? I could have sworn that I did." She smiled up at him and lightly touched his arm. "I think it's about time to head in."

The dinner lasted several hours and the food kept coming, course after course, each paired with a different wine. Chase liked them all, especially the rich Cabernet that was paired with grilled lamb chops. After dessert, they went back outside to stretch their legs and have an after dinner drink. Since Chase was driving, he opted to just have straight coffee. He hadn't really talked much to Rick or David as they were seated at the opposite end of the table. But when Lauren excused herself to go off to the ladies room with Tracy, David and Rick strolled over and Chase felt the shift in the air before they said a word.

Rick spoke first. "Lauren gave me the news that you're passing on the project. I was disappointed and I know David was too." David nodded and stayed quiet, to let Rick continue. "We wanted to give you some time before David goes out to the other guys on his list, to make sure you'd really thought this through. It could be an incredible opportunity for you. For all of us."

Chase felt ambushed, annoyed and oddly flattered all at the same time. But he'd made up his mind and already given David his answer.

"I'm sorry. I appreciate the chance, I do. But, I'm still passing. It's not a good fit for me and I'm pretty busy with work as it is. I'm sure you won't have any trouble finding someone else."

David Wentworth laughed. "No, we won't. I'm disappointed that it won't be you, given your relationship with Lauren and Rick. I like to work with people I know and trust. But I do think you'll regret it. This is going to be huge. Huge!"

Lauren walked up as David finished talking and looked around excitedly. "Are we celebrating something? Did Chase change his mind?" Now it was his turn to feel disappointment. Lauren had known the two of them were going to approach him again. It had put him in an uncomfortable spot and he didn't appreciate it.

"No. We're not celebrating anything. It has been a wonderful night though. Thanks for including me."

"Are you ready to head home?" Lauren asked. Disappointment was evident on her face.

"Sure, I'm ready."

The ride home was quiet and when he pulled onto Lauren's street she was yawning. He was pretty tired himself. It had been a long night, with lots of food and he was ready to fall into bed.

"Aren't you exhausted?" Lauren asked as he pulled in her driveway. He smiled, and knew that was code for 'I just want to go to sleep, alone.'

"I am. Looking forward to crawling into bed and sleeping late tomorrow. Goodnight, Lauren." He leaned over to give her a kiss and it was over in a second.

"Goodbye, Chase."

11

Kristen suffered from severe phone phobia. The thought of calling someone she didn't know or even someone she did know that wasn't a close friend or family member filled her with dread. It always had, and she didn't know why it was so terrifying but it was. So, instead of calling all the local galleries to see if they were interested in taking some of her new paintings, she preferred to drop in, say hello and wait for them to ask if she had anything new. Most of them knew her by now, so it was usually an easy conversation.

She always put the visits off as long as she could, but the paintings were piling up in her studio and although she had a healthy savings account, it could use some replenishing. She had plans to meet her mother and sisters for lunch at Black-Eyed Susan's, and figured she might as well go early and stop by a few of the galleries first, including Andrew's. His was the newest, but he'd been nice enough to give her a solo show recently and she'd gotten to know him and really liked him. He was as passionate about art as she was and they'd had some lively discussions.

She knew that her mother and sisters were disappointed when she'd gone back to Sean, especially after just starting to date Andrew. She didn't blame them. Andrew was everything that Sean wasn't, humble, creative and down to earth and very good at what he did. Andrew loved art and he had a good eye. He wasn't an artist himself but he had a knack for discovering new talent.

Andrew was unfortunately, off the market. After Kristen had made the choice to go back to Sean, Andrew had been disappointed but rebounded quickly and met Nicole, an elementary school teacher and Nantucket native. Kristen knew Nicole and liked her. Given their personalities, she thought they'd be a good match. She'd had a twinge of regret when she stopped dating Andrew, but she knew if she didn't at least try with Sean, she'd regret it.

And she wasn't surprised at all to learn that Andrew and Nicole were getting serious. She really was happy for them. She headed into town an hour before she was due to meet her sisters and mother and stopped by two galleries and chatted with the owners. Both of them said they'd love to take a few of her paintings, which was good news. She saved Andrew's gallery for last as it was just a short walk to Black-Eyed Susan's, so could head over there when they finished up.

Andrew wasn't in the gallery when she first stepped inside. There was an older woman that she vaguely recognized. She looked to be about her mother's age. The woman smiled when she saw Kristen.

"Hello, dear. You're one of the Hodges girls, right? I know your mother from the Garden Club. I hope she's well? Haven't seen her in a while."

"Yes, I'm Kristen. She's good, she's just been busy with the bed-and-breakfast."

"Oh, that's right. What a clever idea that was. I always thought it would be fun to run a bed-and-breakfast myself. Maybe someday. Are you looking for anything particular?"

"I'm looking for Andrew, actually. Is he in?"

"I'm right here." Andrew came walking out of the back office and smiled when he saw Kristen. He walked over and gave her a big hug.

"I thought I recognized that voice. How are you? Come on back and we can chat."

"I'm good, thanks." She followed Andrew to his office and was surprised to see someone else there.

Tyler was sitting in one of the chairs facing Andrew's desk. He stood when they walked in.

"Kristen, you remember my brother, Tyler?"

"Of course."

Tyler didn't say a word, just barely nodded in her direction and turned to his brother. "I'll leave you two to talk. Catch you later." His words were short and clipped and he left so abruptly that Kristen was surprised. It was like he was in a bad mood.

"Sorry, about my brother. He's having a rough day. He's on his way to a meeting."

"A meeting?"

"Alcoholics Anonymous. He goes to meetings regularly but sometimes, during stressful times, he seeks out additional ones. It helps."

"I hope everything is ok?"

"It will be. Each year it gets easier. It's his anniversary. They've been divorced for a little over three years."

"Oh, I didn't know he was married." She'd just assumed that he'd always been single like her.

"He married young, right after college. And they were good for a long time. Until he started having problems with his drinking. He'd always been a social drinker, like all of us, but it turned into more than that, and he didn't get help until it was too late."

"Too late?"

His wife, Taylor, was done and asked for a divorce. That's when he hit rock bottom. But we staged an intervention and got him into a program and to give him credit, he's been sober since."

"His wife wouldn't take him back, even after getting sober?"

Andrew shook his head. "There was too much water under the bridge for them at that point. They'd grown apart before the divorce. She's already remarried. At least they never had kids."

"That's good, I guess," Kristen agreed.

"He put the time to good use. He started writing seriously when he got out of rehab. Tyler was a journalist before that and a good one, but he'd always dreamed of writing a book, and with Taylor gone, he had a lot of time on his hands. It became an addiction that replaced the drinking."

"I had no idea." Kristen felt for him. She still had moments of sadness over ending things with Sean, even though she knew it was the best decision for her. She couldn't imagine the level of sadness Tyler must be feeling.

"I'm only telling you this because you're living so close to him now. I like that someone I know and trust is nearby."

"You worry about him." Kristen could tell that their bond was strong.

Andrew nodded. "He's my older brother, but yeah, I worry when he is going through a rough time. I just want him to be safe, and happy. I'm glad I was able to convince him to move here."

"I'm glad too. Manhattan is a fun place to visit, but even with all those people I'd feel lonely if I was there by myself."

"Please don't mention to Tyler that I shared any of this with you. He's pretty private."

"Of course not."

"So, what brings you in to see me today? I hope you might have more paintings?"

"As a matter of fact, I do."

LISA WAS LOOKING FORWARD to having lunch with her girls, though actually it was breakfast that Black-Eyed Susan's served until one and then they reopened for dinner. She and the girls all loved to occasionally meet there for the best sourdough French toast and Susan's special grits with ham, and hollandaise. Lisa made sure to get her morning walk along the beach in so she could indulge. It had been harder than usual though. The walk had seemed longer even though it was the same distance that she always did. She wondered if maybe she was coming down with something. But after, a long, hot shower, she felt more herself.

When she arrived at the restaurant, Abby and Kate were already outside in line. There was almost always a line there in the summer months. It was a small restaurant with really good food. Kristen was the last to arrive, a few minutes late, but with a smile on her face and Lisa guessed that her gallery meetings had gone well.

"Sorry I'm late. Andrew and I were catching up. I didn't get her name, but there's a woman who works there that knows you from the Garden Club."

"Oh, I think that's Missy Lewis. She mentioned last time I saw her that she was working part-time at one of the galleries. I didn't realize it was Andrew's."

They didn't have to wait too much longer before they were seated and put their orders in. They always got the same thing. The girls all had the sourdough French toast with the orange Jack Daniels butter and cinnamon pecans. Lisa had the veggie scramble and her side of smothered grits.

Kristen gave them the good news that all the galleries had wanted more paintings from her. Lisa was so proud of Kristen that she'd been able to support herself with her painting. It hadn't happened quickly. Until several years ago, she'd always worked hard waitressing and other part-time jobs, just enough to pay the bills and to give enough free time for her painting.

"Andrew had an interesting idea for me. He suggested that I put up a web page and sell prints of some of my best paintings and maybe other products too like greeting cards or coffee mugs. I told him that seemed like a lot of work, but he said it's really not. What do you all think?" Kristen looked intrigued but apprehensive.

"I think it's a fantastic idea!" Kate said. "There are all kinds of places online to sell creative stuff, shops on Etsy for instance or different places where they will make whatever you want, mugs, shirts, etc. and print your design. I could research it a little for you if you like?"

"If you wouldn't mind, that would be great." Kristen sounded relieved. She was the least tech savvy of the family.

"Mind? I love that kind of thing. Doing Mom's advertising is fun for me. A nice change from the writing."

"How is that going?" Abby asked.

Lisa watched Kate's face carefully as she answered. She'd sensed that Kate had been a little stressed recently with her writing, so she didn't ask how it was going the last time she saw her daughter.

But Kate laughed and didn't seem to mind the

question at all. "It's going good now. Really well actually. It wasn't a few weeks ago. I was pretty miserable and wondered if I was ever going to be able to finish another book again. But I had lunch with Philippe and he gave me some great advice that worked and now I'm back on track."

"That's great honey. If you girls will excuse me, I'm going to run to the ladies room. I'll be right back." Lisa stood and winced when shooting pain ran through her knees and the soles of her feet. She felt a bit like an old woman as she slowly made her way to the back of the restaurant. If she moved too quickly, all her joints seemed to hurt and she was so stiff. She thought once again that she must be coming down with something. Hopefully whatever it was would blow by quickly.

When she returned to the table and carefully sat down, the girls all exchanged worried glances.

"Mom, what's wrong with you? Did you pull a muscle or something? You look like you're in pain?" Kate's voice matched the worry that was on all three faces.

"I must be coming down with something. I haven't felt myself the past week. All my joints feel so stiff and painful." She smiled and made a joke of it. "Maybe I'm just getting old."

"Very funny," Abby said. "You should go see Dr.

Casey this week. When was the last time you had a checkup?"

"I'm due, actually. Maybe I will see if they can fit me in this week or next and I'll mention it to her when I see her. Hopefully, I'll be feeling fine by the time I go in."

12

When Kristen got home, she went to paint for a few hours, but found it difficult to get into the zone. She was sleepy and full from the carb heavy meal, and she ate every last crumb. She finally gave in and put her brush down and did something she rarely did. She sprawled on the soft sofa in her sunroom and closed her eyes for just a few minutes.

She woke an hour later, feeling disoriented at first but once she got up, she felt refreshed, but still not really in the mood to paint. She took a walk outside to get the mail and glanced at the cottage next door. Tyler's car was there, so he was home. She thought about what Andrew told her earlier and she wondered how he was doing. She wanted to do something to help, but didn't know what she could do. Or what would even be welcome. Tyler was a very private person.

As she walked back inside, an idea came to her. Kristen wasn't much of a cook, but she had a sweet tooth and loved baking. And everyone raved about her peanut butter chocolate chip cookies. She hadn't made them in ages and she was pretty sure she had all the ingredients on hand.

A quick check of the kitchen showed that she had everything she needed and she got to work, pulling out her pretty turquoise Kitchen-Aid mixer. She followed the recipe on the back of the Nestle Semi-Sweet chocolate chips bag and the only change she made was to add a heaping large spoonful of creamy peanut butter. It did something magical to the cookies, gave them a hint of peanut flavor and made them delicate and delicious so they melted in your mouth. And of course she had to sample the batter, even though it supposedly wasn't good for you. It was irresistible.

An hour later, she had dozens of warm cookies resting on paper towels all over her kitchen counters. She found a plastic container, lined it with a paper towel and filled it with several dozen cookies leaving just a handful for herself. And then before she could lose her nerve, she walked over to Tyler's cottage and rang his doorbell. It took a long time for him to come to the door and she was just about to ring it again when he opened it and looked surprised when he saw her.

"Oh! I thought you were the UPS man. I'm expecting a package."

"Well, I do have a package for you. Hopefully more exciting than what UPS is bringing." She held out the container of cookies. "Peanut butter chocolate chip. I made a huge batch and shouldn't eat them all. I thought you might like some. Consider it a welcome to the neighborhood." The words came out in a rush. It had seemed like a good idea at the time but now she was feeling intimidated by his silence.

Finally, he took the container and a slow smile spread across his face.

"I know that Andrew told you what today is."

Kristen didn't know what to say to that so she said nothing. "Do you want to come in for a minute? Your container is still warm. Did these just come out of the oven?"

She nodded. "Are you sure? I don't want to interrupt your writing."

"I can take a cookie break. I'm almost done for the day, anyway."

"Okay then." She followed him inside, to his kitchen where he opened the container, found a paper plate and put a few cookies on it.

"Let's go to the porch. There's a good breeze out there. It's where I've been working." His porch was identical to hers, but instead of a fluffy white sofa, his was a deep navy velour, so dark it was almost black. He sat on one side of it and she settled on the other. He put the plate of cookies between them. She looked around the room and noticed a standing desk that faced outside with a nice view of the yard and flowering bushes.

"How much did he tell you?" Tyler asked as he reached for a cookie.

Kristen hesitated, unsure how much she should share as Andrew had said not to say anything.

"It's okay. He gave me the heads up that he told you. I think he felt bad that he told you as much as he did. But, I understand why he did, since we're neighbors and all. And he worries."

"He said it was a hard day for you, and the third anniversary of your divorce."

Tyler nodded. "He got part of it wrong. It's an emotional day, but not for the reason he thinks. Taylor and I were heading toward divorce, anyway. My drinking just made it happen sooner rather than later. She did me a favor filing when she did. I don't have any hard feelings toward her. I wish her well."

Kristen reached for a cookie and took a bite, listening as he continued to explain.

"It's just a big day. It's hard to really understand if you haven't suffered from addiction, but it's a milestone and it brings up all kinds of feelings and urges."

"You still want to have a drink?" Kristen asked.

He laughed. "I always want a drink. I loved drinking. But I hate it too, because you know how you can go out with your friends and have a few drinks or even just one and then go home?"

She nodded.

"Well, I can't do that. There is no such thing as one drink. If I open a bottle of wine, I'll drink the whole bottle, or two bottles. Once I start, I have to drink it all. Have you ever gone to a restaurant and not finished your drink because you were full?"

"All the time. Especially if I order a second glass when my meal is served. I almost never finish and leave a half a glass or more."

Tyler groaned. "See, I could never do that. Ever. There's no such thing as just a little for me. I wish there was."

Kristen tried to imagine what that would be like, and how hard it must be to not drink when everyone around you was socializing and having a cocktail. Before she could stop herself, she asked the question that she was most curious about and that was none of her business, at all.

"Have you relapsed at all, since you stopped?"

He smiled. "No. Not yet. I've come close a few times. But I know what will happen and it's not worth it. When I feel like that and it happens once or twice a year, I go find a meeting fast."

"And that helps?"

"It does. Because they've all been there. And I don't want to let them down. I don't want to let Andrew or anyone down. But most of all me." They were both quiet for a minute. Tyler reached for another cookie and inhaled it in two bites. "These are good. Thank you." He looked out the window and then at Kristen. "My life was a mess before I went into rehab. It was dark and ugly. It's good now, and I don't intend to go back there."

"I don't want you to go back there either. If I can be of any help, I'm right next door."

"You're sweet. You don't have to worry though. This is my one dark day for the year and now it's brighter. I made it to a meeting, saw my brother and now I have cookies. It doesn't get much better than that."

Kristen laughed. "I'm not much of a cook, but I can manage cookies now and then."

"How are you doing? You're fresh off a breakup, any regrets?"

"No. We broke up once before and it was harder that time. That's when I met your brother and we went out. But I wasn't in the right mind to be with anyone else. It was too soon and then Sean finally did what I'd asked and filed for divorce. He was separated when I met him and I thought then that divorce was right around the corner. This time, it was easier as I was more sure of my decision. I still miss him sometimes but not enough to want him back."

"That makes sense. It's good to take time to just be by yourself. You'll know when you're ready to get back out there again."

"I hate the sound of that. I'm in no hurry."

"You will be, when the time is right. It can be fun to date a little, meet new people."

She smiled. "You sound like you're speaking from experience. Have you met anyone interesting yet here?"

"Interesting, yes. I've gone out with Andrew a few times and he knows people everywhere we go, so I've met a few women. One actually asked me out that night we saw you at Millie's. Her name is Violet and we're supposed to meet for a drink later this week."

"Violet? I think I know her. She's a bit older than us?" That was an understatement. Kristen wasn't exactly sure of Violet's age, but she was no spring chicken.

"I think she said she was twenty-nine, so odds are she's a little older. She seemed nice enough and I don't know many people here yet, so I'm happy to meet her for a drink."

"That doesn't bother you?" Kristen asked.

"What?"

"Going to a bar, meeting someone for drinks?"

"It did at first. The first year was hard. I tried it maybe once or twice. But now I don't mind at all. I can have an O'Doul's which is actually a pretty decent non-alcoholic beer. And it's kind of interesting to be completely sober in a bar with people drinking all around you. Did you know a big percentage of bartenders are alcoholics?"

"I never thought about it, but it doesn't surprise me, now that you mention it. Thinking back to the restaurants I worked at, I rarely saw the bartenders drink off-hours."

Tyler yawned and Kristen realized she'd been there for close to an hour. The time had flown, but she knew it had been a long day for him.

"I should probably get going and let you get back to your writing." She stood and Tyler yawned again and stood too.

"I think I'm done writing for the day, but I am pretty tired. I think it's going to be an early night. I do appreciate the cookies. Thank you for bringing them by."

Kristen smiled. "You're welcome. Have fun on your date with Violet," she teased him.

"I'll let you know how it goes." He walked Kristen to the door and watched until she let herself into her porch. She looked back and he waved as she locked her door behind her.

13

C hase didn't make coffee Sunday morning until just after eleven. He and Lauren slept in after a late night out with friends at the Chicken Box. It had been a good night, lots of fun and his irritation with Lauren had disappeared as soon as she called him Saturday afternoon to see if he wanted to go out with her and her friends. She was in a great mood and beautiful as ever and he was hopeful again that maybe this could turn into something more serious.

He added two sugars and a splash of half and half to her coffee, gave it a stir and handed it to her as she was relaxing on his living room sofa, flipping through the real estate section of the local paper. She was wearing one of his old t-shirts and it was huge and looked adorable on her.

"Are you hungry? I have donuts or…I guess donuts is it. They're good ones though."

She laughed. "No, on the donut, thanks. The coffee is fine."

He poured himself a cup, grabbed two of the sugary cinnamon donuts and sat next to her. Lauren took a sip of coffee and looked around the room and then shook her head.

"I don't know how you can stand this place. It's so small. You should get yourself a real house. I could help you find something."

"I don't mind it here. It's a place to sleep. I've told you before, I'm not in a hurry. I want to wait until I can afford to do what I want to do. To build my dream house exactly the way I want it."

Lauren narrowed her eyes, "When will that be?"

"I'm not sure. Probably not for a few more years at least. You know how expensive everything is here."

"You could probably qualify for a Covenant home, that would at least be better than this place."

"I make too much to qualify. I have for a few years now. It's a great program, but I don't want to be restricted and with what I do, my house could also be great advertising for the kind of quality I'm capable of."

"True, but that could be five to ten years from now. That's so long. I know you already said no, but it's probably not too late to still do the condo project. That might get you where you want to be sooner."

Chase was sick of hearing about David Wentworth's project. "I'm not changing my mind and I don't want to discuss it again."

"Okay, fine. It was just a suggestion." Lauren sulked as she sipped her coffee.

Chase had been looking forward to a relaxing day with her, but he didn't like the mood she was in. Still, he tried to shift the focus. "What do you feel like doing this afternoon? Want to go see a movie or something?"

Lauren yawned and turned another page. "I don't think so." Her tone was frosty. "I think I'm just going to head home soon."

"Oh? I thought we'd spend the day together."

"I have so much laundry to do and errands to run. It's going to be a busy week." Lauren stood and brought her coffee cup to the kitchen, rinsed it and left it in the sink. She went into the bedroom and came out a few minutes later in her jeans and a sweater, with her designer purse over her shoulder.

"Last night was fun," Chase said as he walked her to the door and pulled her in for a goodbye kiss. She allowed it for just a few seconds and then pulled away and took a step backwards. "It was fun. I'll talk to you later."

He watched her walk to her car and drive off

before he closed the door and added more coffee to his mug. He was feeling a little deflated. They'd had such a good night and he'd been planning to hang out with her all day and just relax. But, as it turned out Lauren wasn't one to sit around and relax. Not with him anyway. He had the whole day ahead of him now and he wondered what to do with himself.

His mother usually had Sunday dinner for whoever was around but he knew that she and Rhett had gone off-island to Boston the night before to see a Red Sox game and have dinner in the North End. He decided to give Abby a call. He hadn't hung out much with his baby sister lately.

She answered on the first ring and invited him over to spend the afternoon watching movies and catching up.

He showered and changed and arrived at his sister's house an hour later. He didn't see Jeff's car in the driveway and asked about him once he was inside.

"He's golfing with his brother. So, your timing is perfect. We have all afternoon to eat junk food, watch Netflix and solve all the world's problems."

Chase laughed and gave her a big hug. "I've missed you. We need to do this more often."

"Yes, we do. But you've been busy with a certain someone lately. How is that going? Wait don't tell me until we're settled in the living room. I need a bowl of ice cream, want to join me?"

"Sure, load me up." Abby filled two bowls full of this week's favorite flavor, caramel fudge ripple, and they got comfortable in the living room.

"Okay, so fill me in, how is everything going with Lauren? Are you madly in love? Or is she a bitch and you're breaking up?"

Chase laughed again. "Somewhere in the middle I guess. It depends on the day. She has her moments. She was pushing me hard still to do that condo project."

"The one you already turned down?"

"Yeah. They brought it up Friday night at the wine tasting we went to at the Wauwinet."

"How was that? Was it amazing? I've never been there and have heard it's so elegant."

"It is. The food and wine was incredible. But I didn't expect that Lauren's brother Rick and David Wentworth would be joining us. It was fine until it was almost over and we were outside. That's when they brought it up again. Maybe they thought they'd get me liquored up and I'd agree. But I was driving, so I didn't drink as much as the rest of them. Lauren was pretty disappointed too, I could tell."

"She invited you to that dinner, right?" Abby asked.

"She did and I wasn't happy when I dropped her off and she was pretty annoyed too. I didn't expect to see her for the rest of the weekend, but then she called the next day and invited me out to go hear some music at the Chicken Box."

"How was that?"

"It was really fun, actually. We had a great night and slept late this morning at my place. I thought we'd spend the day together, but she brought it up again after telling me my place was too small and I really should buy something."

Abby laughed. "And I suppose she offered to find the perfect house for you?"

"She did actually. And when I said no yet again, she suddenly had things to do and went home."

"I'm sorry, Chase. I know you really like her."

"She can be a great girl and there's just something about her. She's gorgeous, but it's more than that."

Abby laughed. "It's lust, pure and simple. You're physically attracted to her. But that won't last if you don't like her as a person."

Chase thought about that for a moment. He wasn't ready to give up on Lauren yet. "I think maybe it will be okay now that she knows I'm definitely out for that project. I told her not to bring it up again."

"Hmmm. It's too bad you're not attracted to Beth, she'd be a great match for you."

"My Beth?"

Abby laughed. "Yes, your Beth. Although it might

be too late now, anyway. She had a date the other night and it went well. They're going out again."

Chase pictured Beth in her navy blue top and that red hair. She was a pretty girl. There was no denying that.

"No kidding. Good for her. Beth is great. I've just never thought of her that way. Plus, she works for me, so that wouldn't be a good idea. Could really awkward if it didn't work out."

"Or it could be really amazing if it did." Abby smiled as she polished off the last of her ice cream. "But, like I said, it's probably too late now, anyway. She seems to like this new guy."

"And I'm not ready to give up on Lauren yet. I still think there's potential there."

"Maybe there is. I hope so, if that's what you want. I just want you to be happy, with someone that will love you for you."

Chase grinned. "Thanks. I think that's pretty much what everyone wants."

"You have to go out with him at least one more time. To really give him a chance and see if there could be something there. Has he kissed you yet?" Abby asked. Beth was on the phone in her office eating lunch which was just soup because she had a dinner date with Ben after work. But she really didn't feel like going.

"No, he hasn't. We've gone out twice now and he's been a perfect gentleman. It's just that there's something missing. I don't really want him to kiss me, so I said goodbye, gave him a hug and pulled away before it could turn into anything else."

"You had a nice time though?"

Beth sighed. "Yes, very nice. He's a good dinner companion. We ended up splitting nachos on our first date, at Millie's, and Sunday night he took me to Black-Eyed Susan's and we brought our own bottle of wine."

"Oh, that's kind of fun. They don't serve alcohol right?"

"Yeah, it's BYOB only and he did pick out a good bottle of wine."

"Beth, he sounds pretty great so far."

"I know. He's a catch, but I don't think he's the one for me."

"Well, maybe third time will be the charm. Remember what happened with Linda?"

"That's true. And to think Linda tried to push Paul on me!" Beth had gone to the Cape with their mutual friend Linda years ago for a set-up of sorts. Linda's friend Kevin wanted her to meet his brother Paul and she didn't want it to be a date-date, so they agreed to just all meet up for drinks and go from there. But the ferry to the Cape was sold out and they had to wait for the next one, so by the time they got to the pub in Dennis Port, Paul and Kevin had had several drinks and Paul was kind of a jerk, making jokes he thought were funny but they weren't. Now that Beth knew Paul well, she realized that he was just extremely nervous that night and was trying too hard.

As the weeks went by Linda saw Paul a few more times when everyone got together for cookouts or beach days. She even tried to fix Beth up with him at one point but Beth thought she was crazy and told her if she thought he was so great she should date him. It wasn't until Linda's sister met Paul and thought he was cute and said so, that suddenly Linda realized he was the one for her and told her sister he was off limits. They got married two years later.

"I'm not sure this is the same though. Ben hasn't done anything to push me away." *He's just not Chase.* But she realized she had to give up on that dream. If Chase was remotely interested, it would have happened already. Clearly she wasn't his type. And he was head over heels for Lauren.

"I'll give it my best shot. Maybe I'll even let him kiss me this time."

"Good. You never know, you might be surprised by sparks after all!"

Beth laughed. "I'll call you tomorrow."

"You'd better. I have no life now, I'll be waiting for all the details."

"Goodbye." Beth was still chuckling as she ended the call, then turned as the door opened. She figured it was the mailman and was surprised when Chase walked in.

"Would you believe I left my phone here this morning?" Chase often stopped by the office long before Beth arrived, to pick up any plans or paperwork he might need before heading out to the worksites.

Beth glanced toward his office. The door was ajar and sure enough, she could see his phone sitting on top of a pile of papers. He went and got it and slipped it into his back pocket.

"I won't be back later. I'm going to some chamber of commerce thing with Lauren so I need to go home a little early and shower." He stopped and took a good look at Beth's outfit and she felt herself start to blush. She had dressed up more than usual for this date. She wanted to look good and truth be told, she wanted to see if Chase would notice, but when he did, she wasn't quite prepared for it.

"You look really pretty, Beth. Did you do something different with your hair?"

"I used a straightener on it, so it might look a little shiny."

"That's it. So, you're going out again with that guy? Abby mentioned that things are going well so far."

"She did?" Beth wondered what Abby was up to. It wasn't like her to gossip like that.

"Yeah, and I was glad to hear it. You deserve a great guy, Beth." His phone vibrated and he glanced down at it. "Gotta go. Have fun tonight and I'll see you tomorrow."

THE DATE WAS FINE. Ben met her at the movie theater and they shared a pizza after. During the movie, he had his arm around her and lightly resting on her shoulder. And she felt nothing other than the urge to smack it away, but she did nothing. Their hands brushed a few times when they reached for the popcorn at the same time, and again nothing.

After the movie and the pizza, Ben walked her to her car and when he tried to gently kiss her goodnight, she let him. And she still felt nothing. Ben however seemed to think things were going splendidly and promised to call to go out again. She knew though, that there wouldn't be a fourth date, and she dreaded having to tell him, but she simply couldn't go out with him again, it wouldn't be fair to either of them.

14

Paige loved Bailey dearly, but the little hellion was not only into everything, he'd also started to sharpen his claws on her favorite tan sofa. That had to stop. She certainly wasn't going to do anything as drastic as declawing him, but maybe a nice scratching post could be a solution. There were five or six to choose from at Geronimo's Pet Store and she'd just selected one and was going to bring it to the register when she heard a familiar voice behind her.

"So yours has discovered his claws too?" Paige turned to see Peter Bradford walking toward her.

"He's a terror," she confided.

"Mine too. That's the one you decided on?" Paige nodded and he grabbed one too and followed her to the register. They chatted while they were in line and Paige learned that Peter was a fan of blues music.

"There's actually a concert downtown this Saturday. It's a blues band I've seen before and they're really good. If you're not busy, maybe you'd like to go with me?"

Paige was so surprised by the invitation that she didn't hesitate and gladly accepted. She wasn't exactly sure if he meant it to be a date, but she liked Peter and looked forward to seeing him again.

"I'll call you tomorrow to make a plan for Saturday," he said when they reached their respective cars in the lot.

"That sounds good."

PAIGE WAS in a good mood as she drove home. The unexpected encounter and invitation had lifted her spirits. Not that they'd need much lifting, but she'd been feeling a little down lately. All of her friends were coupled up. She didn't mind being alone, and was used to it by now, but she'd had a taste in Florida of how nice it could be to have someone around, another presence in the house. Bailey was great, but it wasn't the same.

When she pulled into her driveway, she saw a cardboard box on Violet's front porch and wondered if it was the cheesecakes she'd mentioned. Violet had left earlier in the day, taking the first flight out to New York City. The Nantucket airport was small, but it had direct flights to Boston and New York City and every year the number of private planes that flew into Nantucket increased.

She brought the cat scratch pole inside and set it up near the sofa. She sat back and waited for Bailey to investigate. It didn't take long. He came bounding over to where she sat on the sofa, looked at her quizzically and then walked up to the scratching pole. He sniffed it and tentatively touched a paw to the scratching surface. After a few minutes, he was scratching happily and rolling around on the rug. While he was entertaining himself, Paige grabbed Violet's key and went next door to bring the cheesecakes inside.

The box held four cheesecakes and was heavy. She fished out the right key, opened the door and went inside. She was surprised by how spotless Violet's home was. There was zero clutter and nothing was out of place. It almost didn't look lived in. But in the kitchen by the phone, she saw a stack of mail and a small note-book. She put the box of cheesecakes on the counter and rummaged around to find a pair of scissors to cut the packing tape and open the box. She carefully removed each cheesecake and stacked them on Violet's bottom shelf where she had made room for them.

When she returned to take the box out to the trash,

she saw that the small notebook had fallen off the counter and landed face side up. She bent down to pick it up and something caught her eye and even though she knew it was none of her business, she took a closer look. It appeared to be some kind of register, a listing of names and dollar amounts. No first names, just first initial and last name and it was the first name that had caught her eye.

T. Smith, $2,000. It was written in pen and there was a slash through it. Unlike the other names listed, and there were a dozen or so, spanning several months with varying amounts from $500 to $5,000. None of those entries had slash marks.

Paige told herself that Smith was a common name, and the T wasn't necessarily Tom. But, the date of the entry matched the weekend that Tom Smith went missing. When she picked up the small book, a piece of paper fluttered from the pages to the floor. Paige picked it up and saw that it was a check, from a Thomas Smith and the amount and the date matched the entry in the book. It appeared as though there was some truth to the rumors about Violet. But the big question was what actually happened that night? And why hadn't she cashed the check?

Dr. Andrea Casey had a cancellation and was able to squeeze Lisa in a few days after her girls demanded that she make an appointment. The whole family saw Dr. Casey. She was about Lisa's age and no-nonsense. She was baffled by Lisa's symptoms though.

"Nothing seems obviously wrong. All your vitals are good. But I don't like what you're experiencing. There's always the possibility of Lyme disease, but usually you would have noticed the bite. It's a quite distinctive red bull's eye pattern.

"I would have noticed that," Lisa agreed. "And we don't have any pets that would bring ticks in."

"You can get them just by walking outside. I think, to be safe, we'll include a check for that in your blood work. I'll have the results either later today or tomorrow and we'll go from there. Until then, make sure you get plenty of rest."

Lisa agreed and when she got home, after throwing a chicken and a few potatoes in the oven to roast, she grabbed a magazine and went to lie down for just a few minutes. She was bone tired, utterly exhausted and felt like she could sleep for hours. But she set her phone alarm for one hour and fell fast asleep.

She woke to the wonderful aroma of roast chicken with a hint of lemon and garlic. It was a simple dish to prepare, she just sliced a lemon, and stuffed it in the chicken cavity along with a few cloves of garlic and then drizzled olive oil and melted butter over the chicken along with a sprinkling of salt and pepper. She cut the potatoes in half and added them to the same pan, tossing them in a bit of olive oil, salt, pepper and rosemary. She'd invited Rhett for dinner and he would be home shortly.

The chicken had been in for a little over an hour and it looked and smelled done. She pulled the roasting pan out of the oven and set it on the stove top to rest. A short rest would make the meat even juicier. She tented it with a big sheet of aluminum foil to keep the heat in and microwaved some broccoli for a vegetable. Normally, she'd have a glass of wine as well, but it didn't appeal to her in the least at the moment and she had a feeling it would send her right back to sleep.

As she was taking the broccoli out of the microwave, the phone rang and the caller ID showed that it was Dr. Casey's office.

"Lisa? This is Andrea Casey. I have the results of your blood work and everything looks normal, except that you do apparently have Lyme disease. I'm glad we tested for it. It's rare that we don't see the bulls-eye bite, but it does happen. I've called in a prescription for the antibiotic Doxycycline to your pharmacy."

When she hung up the phone, Lisa immediately

called Rhett to see where he was and if he wouldn't mind picking up her prescription on the way home.

"Your timing is good, I'll be going by Stop and Shop in about five minutes. Did they figure out what's wrong with you?"

"Lyme disease of all things. I'll have to be more careful when I walk through some of the seagrass on the way to the beach."

"At least you know why you feel so lousy. I'll be home in about fifteen minutes. Do you want to go out to eat? I don't want you to have to cook."

Lisa laughed. "The cooking is all done. We're just having roast chicken."

"I love your chicken. Maybe I'll see you in ten minutes," he teased.

An hour or so later, when they were finished eating, Rhett insisted on doing the dishes while Lisa packaged up the leftovers and put them in the refrigerator. It was a beautiful night and they decided to sit out on the front porch for a while. Lisa sipped a hot tea with lemon and honey and Rhett had a decaf coffee. They sat side by side in the soft, cushioned love seat that glided back and forth.

They chatted for about a half hour and then Lisa couldn't keep the yawns away. Rhett saw it and took her hand and gave it a gentle squeeze.

"Have you looked into hiring anyone to help you yet with the cleaning?"

She shook her head. "No, not yet. I know I should. It took me twice as long today and I'm sure it will tomorrow too." All the rooms were full and three of them were turning over the next day, so she'd need to strip the beds and wash the sheets and remake the beds. It wasn't hard work, but it was time-consuming and just thinking about it made her tired.

"Can I help?"

Lisa laughed as an image of Rhett making the beds came to mind. "You want to clean the rooms?"

"No. But I don't want you to either. And I can probably make a call and get someone who could do it for you."

"Really? That would be heaven. I thought I'd have to post an ad and interview people. I don't even have the energy for that, to be honest."

"I think I know someone who can hook us up." Rhett searched his phone until he found the number he wanted and called it.

"Roger, it's Rhett. I wonder if you might be able to help us out. Any chance you could get someone out to the Beach Plum Cove Inn tomorrow morning to clean a few rooms?"

There was a moment of silence and then Rhett spoke

again, "5 rooms, a few need new sheets and if the person wants steady work for the next month or two, we can give it to them. Alright, see what you can do. Thanks."

"Who is Roger?" Lisa asked when Rhett ended the call.

"He's a young man who found me a bartender at the restaurant when I was stuck a few weeks ago. He runs a referral network of people in the hospitality business, chefs, waitstaff, bartenders, maids, maintenance guys, all kinds of skills and when a need comes in, he makes a few calls and takes care of it. One of our sous chefs does personal chef gigs every now and again through him."

"Do you think he might really be able to find us someone that quickly?" Lisa was hopeful but thought it was unlikely.

"If anyone can do it, Roger can."

Twenty minutes later, Roger called to say that Harriet Johnson would be there the next morning at nine a.m.

"He said she's an experienced chambermaid who is available until December if you need her that long. She goes to Jamaica for the winter."

"That's amazing. Please tell Roger that I said thank you."

When Rhett ended the call, Lisa smiled at him.

"Thank you, too. I was dreading all that cleaning tomorrow."

"I'm glad Roger came through. Now you can rest. How long did the doctor say it would be before you felt better?"

"Just a few weeks."

"Good."

HARRIET JOHNSON ARRIVED at a quarter to nine the next morning and Lisa liked her immediately. She was about Lisa's age, maybe a little younger or older, it was hard to tell. She was small and lean and looked like she did yoga or ballet on a regular basis. Lisa was a little jealous of how toned and firm her arms were. Her black hair was long and fell in dozens of delicate braids that she'd pulled back into a low ponytail. She had a friendly smile, and a faint Jamaican accent.

"How long have you lived on Nantucket?" Lisa asked as she led the way upstairs to show her the rooms and where all the cleaning supplies and linens were.

"Almost twenty years now. I've had my green card for ten years. My husband, Toby and I are both from Jamaica but we met here on Nantucket one Summer and have been together ever since. Oh, and everyone calls me Harry. If you say Harriet, I'm going to think I'm in trouble."

Lisa laughed. "Was that the only time your parents called you that?"

"That's right. Reason I'm available now is because I just got back from Jamaica. My mother had a serious surgery and I wanted to be with her as she lives alone. I ended up being gone for just over a month and the hotel I was working for hired a replacement. I don't blame them, really. But I didn't have any choice."

"No, of course you didn't. I hope your mother is okay now?"

Harry smiled and her whole face lit up. "She's great. The hip replacement surgery was a success and I stayed until she was able to get around easily without help. We usually head back to Jamaica for the winter. So it won't be long before I see her and my sisters again."

Lisa yawned and felt the fatigue wash over her again. Her eyes felt so heavy. She was grateful that Harry was there to help. The other woman looked at her with concern as Lisa leaned against the wall for a second and took a deep breath.

"You look awfully pale. Are you not feeling well?" Harry asked.

Lisa explained about the Lyme disease. "I just

started taking antibiotics, but hopefully it will kick in soon. I hate being so sleepy all the time."

"Well, I think I know where everything is, so why don't you go and rest. When I finish up, I'll knock on your door."

"Okay. Thanks, Harry."

15

Kristen was deep into her world of color, swirling pinks into greens into blues and feeling her way through a painting that had her completely entranced. So, it took her a while to register that in another part of her house, her phone was ringing incessantly. It stopped and then started up again. The mood broken and curious as to who was trying to reach her; she stood and stretched and went to get her phone. There were three missed calls from Kate. No message, which usually meant she just wanted to talk and Kristen should call when she was free.

She dialed Kate's number and her sister picked up on the first ring.

"I totally interrupted you didn't I? You were probably in the zone and I dragged you out of it."

Kristen laughed. "Well, yes. But you called three times, so it must be important. What's up?"

"I want to come over to show you what I did. Your website is up."

"My website? I don't have one."

"You do now! You have coffee mugs, placemats, and several different size prints."

"How did you do that? Aren't you supposed to be writing?"

"Well, yes. But this is what I've been working on when I need to avoid writing. The hardest part for me is starting. But I've been having so much fun getting this done for you. Can you take a break from the painting for a bit?"

"Sure. I've done a lot today, come on over."

Fifteen minutes later, Kate arrived with her laptop and they went into the sunroom and sat side by side on the sofa so Kate could walk Kristen through the site.

"So, there's just one painting for now, as a sample. If you like what I've done, I can include any others that you like. I have my digital camera with me to get really good quality shots."

As Kate showed her sister the site, Kristen was impressed. Kate had taken a picture of one of Kristen's favorite paintings. Jack had bought it at her recent show at Andrew's gallery, and it hung in their living room. And now it was on all the products in Kate's store.

"If you like the look of this, I can make the site live and you can start getting orders immediately."

"It's that quick? How will people find it?"

"I can help with that too. I can put up a few blog posts which will draw organic traffic to the site and we can play around with Facebook and Google ads.

"Sure, go for it. And thank you."

"No problem. This is fun for me." Kate closed the laptop and leaned back on the sofa. "I stopped by Mom's this morning to check on her too."

"How is she feeling?" Kristen had been surprised to find out her mother had Lyme disease of all things. She'd had a friend that got it years ago and she'd been sick for over a year before they figured it out it was Lyme. She was glad that Dr. Casey had thought to check for it even though there was no tell-tale rash.

"She's still tired, but she said it's already better th⸱ it was. Plus, she has help now with the cleaning. I the woman she hired, Harriet, or rather Harᵣ seems nice and the two of them seem like fə already. They were having coffee in the d' with Rhett when I stopped by a little after

"Oh, good. I'm glad she has sor have offered, but I had no idea she fᵣ

"I know. She doesn't like to wᵣ

Kristen smiled. "She said ⸱ same night she heard from

Lyme. I wasn't sure about Rhett at first, but I'm glad he was there to help. They seem to get along great."

"They do," Kate agreed. "How about you? How are you doing? Have you talked to Sean at all?"

"No, he hasn't called, thankfully. I heard he's been spending a lot of time with his soon to be ex-wife again. Maybe they won't go through with it after all."

"I'm so glad you ended it. Any new prospects? Have you seen your new neighbor again? Or his brother?"

Kristen laughed. "Andrew is pretty serious with someone. We're just friends. His brother is interesting. We've chatted a few times. I'm really not looking to date anyone right now, but I think he could use a friend." She told Kate about the day she made cookies and brought them over to Tyler and a little bit about what he was going through.

"That must be hard. I have to confess, I'd miss not having wine. But I can't imagine not being able to stop after a glass or two. That's kind of scary. A lot of writers struggle with addiction. I remember reading tephen King's memoir, On Writing and there was a ssage where he talked about it. He said he'd go out to er and would see people paying their bill and g half glasses of wine behind, unfinished. It was prehensible to him."

sten nodded. "Tyler said something similar. I

think it's like that with him too. Maybe that's part of the reason why his books do so well, his writing is an outlet to channel that frustration and darkness."

Kate nodded. "His books are very dark. Beautifully written though."

"You'll never guess who he's going on a date with?" Kristen had meant to mention it to her sister and totally forgot.

"Who?"

"Violet Jones of all people!"

"Really? That seems like an odd match. Did he ask her out?"

"No. He said he was out with Andrew and she was at the bar they went to, and they got to talking. She invited him out for a drink, and she told him she was twenty-nine!"

"Plus ten, at least," Kate said dryly.

"I don't think there's any serious interest there. just doesn't know many people here and figure' not? Maybe she'll end up a character in on books."

"Well, it will be interesting to see hov do want to chat with him about writir talked to him a few times, why dor' over for dinner one of these nights?'

Kristen laughed. "I don't coo'

"Oh, I don't mean anythir

in the back yard right? Have a cookout, burgers and dogs. I know, we can do a pitch night. I'll bring the clam dip and chips. We haven't played pitch in ages. I can bring the cards too if you need them. And it's the perfect excuse to invite him, we need a fourth."

"That could be fun. Maybe this Friday night?"

"That works for us. I'm pretty sure Jack doesn't have anything planned."

"Okay, I'll see if he's up for it."

"So, he picked you up, insisted on buying dinner and took you to a show, but it wasn't a date?" Lisa laughed and she and Sue exchanged glances as they sat on Lisa's front porch late in the afternoon. There was a slight chill in the air, so Lisa had a fleece throw wrapped around her. The sun was shining brightly though, so they still wanted to sit outside and get some sun. Lisa had been on the antibiotics for a few days and was starting to feel more like herself again and glad that her friends had stopped by to check on her. Paige had just finished telling them about her evening with her Bradford.

"You had a nice time, it seems?" Sue said.

"We did. He's good company. I really don't think of us was thinking of it as a date. I did try to pay my share at dinner. He's just a gentleman. He said he missed going out and doing things."

"Do you think you'll go out again?"

Paige smiled. "We're going to dinner tomorrow night. There's a new restaurant he's been wanting to try. I forget the name of it, but it's Italian."

"Well, I think it's great," Lisa said. "Dating or not dating. If you're enjoying each other's company that's all that matters. See where it goes."

"That's what I'm thinking. I don't think either one of us wants to rush anything."

"Have you seen Violet?" Sue asked.

"Not since she's been back, no." Paige had told them about the check and the notebook with the names and dollar amounts and they were all curious to know more about her relationship with Tom Smith and what had actually happened the night he was dropped off at the hospital.

"Do you think I should tell the police?" Paige asked.

Both Lisa and Sue shook their heads no. "How would you explain that? You were snooping around her kitchen when she wasn't home. She could easily say you planted it there," Lisa said. "Plus, it's none of our business and we don't really know what happened."

"I haven't seen anything in the news or heard anything more around town. I think they just asked a few questions to appease his wife. I mean, I think we all know what likely happened. He overexerted himself somehow when he was with her and she rushed him to the hospital but couldn't bring him in herself because how could she explain that to his wife?" Sue said.

"It's a mess," Paige shook her head. "His poor wife."

"We don't know anything about their relationship though. Not excusing what he may have done, but you never really know what someone's marriage is like. Maybe they were miserable or thinking about divorce."

"Or maybe he was just a jerk," Sue said.

Lisa laughed. "Right, maybe he was. But, my point is we don't know. And we don't know what Violet was doing or why either."

16

"Chase if you're going to the bar, I'll have another chardonnay." Lauren flashed a smile his way before turning back to chat with Tracy and another friend that she'd introduced him to earlier but her name escaped him. They were at the Chicken Box and it was loud. There was a band playing, but he wasn't particularly crazy about them. The place was crowded as usual. Chase wasn't planning to go for another drink anytime soon, but at least it gave him something to do.

He made his way there and stood in line, waiting his turn. His best friend Jim and his wife, Wendy, had come with them too, but they were busy playing pool.

"She crushed me." Chase turned to see Jim right behind him, laughing as Wendy waved on her way back to join the others at their table.

"What do you guys want?" Chase asked as he reached the counter.

"Chardonnay for her, Second Wind IPA for me." Jim held out money, but Chase waved it away. "You can get the next round."

Chase paid and while he was waiting for his change, Jim said, "Hey isn't that the girl that works for you? She's really cute. You know, if she's available, we should set her up with Gerry. He and Meghan broke up last month."

"She's taken," Chase said quickly. Beth looked his way at that moment and smiled when she saw him.

"Too bad. He would have loved her I bet."

Chase handed Jim his drinks and grabbed Lauren's chardonnay and his beer. He was going to go say hello to Beth before delivering the drink, but as he took a step in her direction, a tall, familiar looking guy appeared by her side and put his arm around her. She looked up at him and laughed and the two of them walked off together.

Chase turned around and headed back toward his group's table. He handed Lauren her wine. She was in the middle of telling a story about a recent record sale and didn't even say thank you. She just smiled and continued talking.

"You look like you'd like to be anywhere but here," Jim said.

"I'm just tired. It was a long week and I have a lot on my mind. I probably should have stayed home tonight. But when you said you and Wendy were up for going out, that was hard to pass up." Chase grinned. "You guys don't exactly get out much these days."

Jim laughed. "It's true. It's been ages since we've been here. We've both become homebodies in the past year or so. We just like to relax after a long day, have a nice dinner at home and maybe watch something on Netflix."

"That sounds pretty good, actually."

Jim glanced over at Lauren. "Not exactly her speed though is it?"

Chase chuckled. "Hardly. Lauren would be out socializing every night if she could. She feeds off the energy. The bigger the crowd, the better."

"Well, they say opposites attract, right?"

"Hmmm. I don't know." He lowered his voice. "I was head over heels for her in the beginning. It's been a few months now and I never thought I'd say this, but I'm not so sure anymore."

"Is there someone else you're interested in?" Jim asked.

"What? No. There's no one."

Twenty minutes later, he saw Beth by herself, in line at the bar.

"I'll be right back. I see someone I need to go say hello to."

He walked up to Beth and smiled. "Are you having fun?

"Hey Chase! Yeah, we are having a good time. How about you? Are you here with Lauren?"

He nodded. "There's a group of us over at that table. My buddy Jim and his wife Wendy wanted to go out and that doesn't happen often, so here we are."

"Lauren looks like she's having fun." Chase followed Beth's gaze to the dance floor where Lauren was dancing with some guy he didn't recognize. The whole table was up dancing though as it was a lively song. "She loves to dance," he said. "Who's the guy you're with? He looks familiar. Is he the one you've been dating?"

"That's Ryan Davis. He's an accountant, works for his father's CPA company. He's a nice guy. He's not the one I was dating a few weeks ago."

"Oh? I thought you liked that guy?"

Beth smiled. "He was really nice." A mischievous look came over her face and she leaned in and spoke softly so no one else could hear her. "But I didn't want to kiss him."

Chase didn't know what to say to that. He suddenly felt hot and the image of Beth leaning in to kiss someone flashed through his mind. Finally, he found his voice.

"And what about this guy? Do you want to kiss him?"

"Maybe. It's our first date and I haven't really decided that just yet." Her eyes lit up as she smiled and Chase couldn't help but notice the way her hair danced around her shoulders and how the lipstick she was wearing made her lips seem bigger, pinker, and very kissable. What was wrong with him? Beth was there with someone and he should go see what Lauren was up to.

"Well, good luck then. I should probably head on back. See you on Monday."

"Good night, Chase."

BETH TOOK a deep breath and watched Chase walk back to his table, to Lauren. She sighed and took a sip of her wine. What on earth had come over her to talk to him like that, to share how she felt about kissing? And unless she was imagining it, there was a different sort of vibe between them, almost as if Chase was seeing her for the first time. It was probably all in her head. He was there with Lauren after all.

And she did like Ryan more than Ben. She'd been

about to cancel her membership on the dating app, but then Ryan had messaged her and he seemed interesting. He was better looking in person and even seemed taller than his listed height of six feet so that was a good start to the evening. He'd suggested the Chicken Box as a fun first date because there was music and things to do, pool tables and dart boards, and she'd mentioned in her profile that she loved playing pool even though she wasn't very good at it. Going to the Chicken Box was a nice change from going out to dinner and it gave her a chance to see what he was like in a social environment too.

They'd both run into people they knew and Ryan had introduced Beth to a few of his friends. The only person Beth had recognized was Chase and she was secretly sort of glad that Ryan wasn't around when Chase came over to say hello. It would have felt strange to introduce the two of them, to her anyway. She was sure neither one of them would have had a problem with it.

"Are you ready to try a little pool? It looks like a table just opened up. I can go grab it if you want to play?" Ryan suggested.

"I'd love that."

Beth really did love to play. When she was in college and bartended at a local bar in the afternoons, she learned how to play. Afternoons were slow, as most of the bar's business came in the evenings with the college students. The afternoon crowd was mostly tradesmen. They went to work early and ended their day around two or three and stopped in for a drink with their buddies on the way home. A few of them taught her how to play and she was pretty good for a while, but she played so rarely now that it was like starting all over again.

It was fun though, and after the first game, when Ryan beat her easily, the feel of it came back to her and she played so well that although it was close, she won in the end. Ryan high-fived her. "I thought you said you weren't very good." He laughed as he racked the balls to play one more round.

Beth won again and after that, they joined some of Ryan's friends on the dance floor. Beth noticed that Lauren was up dancing again but not with Chase. She recognized the guy she was dancing with. Troy Merchant was one of the few builders that Chase sometimes lost bids to, as he would underbid to get the work. She glanced over at the table where Chase was sitting. He was deep in conversation and didn't seem to notice or care that Lauren was dancing up a storm without him.

A little after eleven, when the band finished their last song, Beth and Ryan decided to head out. It was a longer than usual first date, but it had been a fun one and she was glad she'd decided to take a risk and go on a date with him.

He walked her to her front door and looked a little unsure as he smiled and said, "I had a really good time tonight. I'd like to go out again, if you're up for it?"

She didn't hesitate. "I'd like that. Thanks for a fun night."

"Would it be okay if I kissed you goodnight?" He asked. Beth wasn't sure if she liked that or was annoyed by it. But she was curious to see if there might be a spark.

"Sure."

He leaned in and softly touched his lips to hers. It was over as soon as it began. There were no sparks, but then it didn't really last long enough for her to determine if there could be.

CHASE SPENT the rest of the weekend thinking about Lauren and how their relationship was going. When he dropped her off after their night at the Chicken Box, she hadn't invited him in and he didn't suggest that she come back to his place. She said she was exhausted and had a busy day on Sunday. She didn't say what she was doing, but he didn't really care anymore. He just agreed that he was tired too and gave her a quick kiss goodnight and said he'd call her tomorrow.

And he did call her on Sunday, after deliberating all day and finally coming to the conclusion that he'd already reached, which was that it was time to end things. He dreaded the conversation as he suspected Lauren was usually the one that decided when to end a relationship. But finally, at around three in the afternoon, he called her. She didn't answer, so he left a message to call him back.

But she never did. It wasn't entirely unlike her not to call back the same day though. Sometimes she took her sweet time getting back to him. It used to make him even more crazy about her, the agony of not knowing if she was into him only seemed to make her more attractive. But now he just wanted closure.

And he got it, but not in the way that he'd imagined. On Tuesday, he stopped for a slice of pizza at lunchtime. He was working on a project near the pier, so walked over to Oath, where they made the slices to order in a super fast oven while you waited. He ate his pizza and on his walk back to work, he saw a couple having a romantic lunch on the pier at Cru. He did a double-take when he got closer and recognized them. Lauren had her hand on the tanned muscled arm of Troy Merchant, the guy she was dancing with at the Chicken Box. Their food was almost untouched as they gazed into each other's eyes. Troy pushed a stand of hair off Lauren's face and tucked it behind her ear and she laughed and ran a finger along his arm.

Chase shook his head and looked away. A few weeks ago, he would have been devastated to see that. He still felt a bit of anger, but more than anything, he felt relief and confirmation that he'd made the right decision. Now he knew why she wasn't calling him back, and given what he just saw, he didn't feel the need to call her again.

Beth wondered if something had happened with Chase and Lauren. He hadn't mentioned her all week and she hadn't called the office once. He'd been quieter than usual until Friday afternoon when he came back to the office early, around three instead of his usual four. He took his mail into his office and she figured he'd be there at least an hour, but twenty minutes later, he walked up to her desk.

"We finished up early today. Can you close up now? Finish whatever you're doing on Monday?"

"Sure. I could do that."

"Good, let's go have an end of the work week drink."

Beth hesitated. "I'd love to, but I have a date with Ryan tonight."

"You have time for one drink? It's only four o'clock. It's been ages since we've done this."

"It has been a while. I guess I could go for one." Now and then, she and Chase used to grab an after work drink and Beth had always loved those nights. She could sit and talk to Chase for hours. They hadn't gone out after work since he started dating Lauren. So she figured something had changed with the two of them.

When they were seated at the tiny pub around the corner from the office with frosty draft beers in front of them, Chase confirmed her suspicions and told her he'd ended things with Lauren.

"I realized it wasn't going to work long-term. We're too different. I dreaded calling her. I was going to suggest meeting so I could do it in person, maybe over coffee or something. But I didn't reach her. And she never called me back.

"So, you never had the conversation?" Beth asked.

"No. I think Lauren was starting to realize I wasn't as easily controlled as she'd hoped. When I said no to that project, I think she started to lose interest. I'm pretty sure she found a replacement already though."

"To date? Or for the project?"

"Hmmm, possibly both, actually. I was thinking dating. I saw the two of them looking very cozy over lunch the other day. They were sitting outside at CRU. Neither one of them saw me. But now that you mention it, it makes sense. They probably approached Troy for the project too."

"It seems more up his alley. I bet he won't think twice about doing the job for less money and using lower quality materials."

"It's probably what he does now. It's the only way it would make sense for him to underbid me on some of those projects. On a few of them, when I knew he was in the running, I really pushed it and bid as low as I possibly could, and it still wasn't enough."

"How are you doing? I know you really liked her?" Beth asked gently.

Chase smiled. "Liked is the key word. The more we spent time together, the more I realized how different we are." He took a sip of his beer, then set the mug down.

"And what about you? You're going on a second date, so the kissing must have been okay?" His tone was light and teasing and Beth was really wishing that she hadn't agreed to go on that second date. She wanted to stay and have another drink with Chase and maybe split a greasy bar pizza and chat for a few more hours. And maybe he'd look at her the way he had the other night, for that split second. But she had said yes and needed to get going soon.

"It was okay, too soon to really know for sure."

Chase nodded. "Yeah, you really need to get to know someone and that takes time."

"Speaking of time, I should probably get going." Beth took another sip of her beer and set the mug down. She reached in her purse for a few dollars, but Chase waved her money away.

"I've got this. Go have fun on your date."

17

Paige was sitting on her living room sofa, with her laptop on her lap, uploading a picture of her latest Hummel figurine to sell on eBay. Bailey kept hopping around behind her, tackling her hair and racing from one end of the sofa to the other. She figured he was about twenty minutes away from collapsing and napping for a few hours. He was like the energizer bunny. He went at full speed until he'd used up every drop of energy and then he'd find a cozy spot to curl up and sleep for a few hours.

She was just about done when both she and Bailey jumped at the sound of a knock at the kitchen door. She wasn't expecting anyone. She went to the door and was surprised to see Violet outside holding what looked like a box of cheesecake. When she opened the door, Violet handed her the box.

"Here you go. If I remember, you said you wanted a bite of my cheesecake, how about a whole box instead?"

"Come on in. That's too much. I can just take a slice and give you back the rest."

"No, I have plenty and besides I'm going to be moving again, and I'm not taking that cheesecake with me."

"You're moving? I thought you were going to stay awhile. Do you have time for a cup of tea? And maybe a slice of cheesecake?"

"I'll pass on the cheesecake, but I'll have a cup of tea with you, sure."

While Paige made the tea, Violet played with Bailey, who loved the attention.

When the tea was ready, Paige brought the cups to the coffee table and took her spot on the sofa again. Violet sat in the matching love seat and took a small sip of the steaming tea.

"So, where are you moving to?" Paige asked.

"Off-Island. I've been here almost fifteen years and I think it's time to go. I'm going to join my sister in Florida. She wants me to work with her and help her run her business. She's been asking me for years and I never wanted to leave Nantucket, but now I'm grateful for the opportunity."

"What kind of business is it?" Paige was curious what Violet would do in Florida.

"She has a temporary staffing business and needs someone to help her manage clients and interview candidates. She said it's fast-paced, so I'll never be bored."

"Well, that does sound promising. But why leave so suddenly?"

Violet sighed. "Nantucket is expensive. I managed to support myself for years, but it was easier when I was younger. I always had generous men that I had... friendships with. Not everyone approves of how I live my life. That's why I moved into this neighborhood. I guess you could say I wore out my welcome in my old one. People talk too much and things get lost in translation. There were some that actually said I was an escort for crying out loud. That's just ridiculous."

"It wasn't any better after you moved here?" Paige asked.

"It was, for a little while. But then there was the situation with Tom."

Paige sat up straighter. "Tom?"

"Smith. The fellow that recently had the heart attacks."

"He was with you?"

"He was." She was quiet for a moment and took another slow sip of her tea.

"I really liked him. We'd been seeing each other for several months. He has some clients on Nantucket and comes over once or twice a month. I knew he was married, but he told me it was as good as over and I believed him. But he never told me about his heart condition and that he was supposed to avoid certain…activities."

"Oh dear…"

"Right. I should have called 911, but I figured I could get him to the hospital just as quickly. So, I drove him there. Brought him in and said I'd be right back. I went home instead. I couldn't go back. For his sake, and for mine. I really didn't think he would die." Her eyes welled up. Paige handed her the box of tissues she kept on the coffee table.

"Did someone recognize you at the hospital?" Paige asked.

Violet sniffed again and then blew her nose so loudly that Bailey jumped.

"No. When that young policeman came around, he said that they'd checked the numbers on Tom's cell phone and mine was the last one he'd dialed, the day he arrived on Nantucket. He'd booked a room at a bed-and-breakfast, but I'm not sure if he ever checked in. He just needed to tell his wife where he was staying."

And now it made sense why he'd prepaid. All he'd

needed was the reservation and the charge on his credit card statement.

"You're not in any kind of trouble from the police?" Paige asked.

"No. They agreed that I didn't do anything wrong. But eventually it will get out that I was with Tom that night and people talk enough about me as it is."

She sipped her tea and looked as though she was thinking about something.

"I feel like I've lost my touch with men lately. I asked that handsome writer, Tyler Black out for a drink and I thought there could be potential there. I am a bit older than him, but I told him I was younger. I'm not sure he believed me though and he didn't mention going out again. With Tom gone, money is getting a little tight again. He gave me a check when he was here. He was always so generous, but I didn't feel right about cashing this one."

Paige sipped her tea and nodded in sympathy. She wasn't sure why Violet was sharing so much, but she guessed that she needed to get it off her chest and talk to someone, and she didn't seem to have many women friends on the island. And maybe it wasn't the sort of thing you'd want to share with your sister.

"Did you sign a lease here? Will it be difficult to get out of?" She wondered.

Violet shook her head. "No, I already talked to them and they have a waiting list of people that want to move in. Reasonably priced housing is a hot commodity here and I was just month-to-month. Thankfully."

"There's really no more good men left here," Violet said. "I met Tom at Rhett's restaurant. I was sort of a regular at the bar there and at one time, when it first opened, I set my sights on Rhett, but he didn't bite. I think he was already getting serious with Lisa Hodges by then. You know, there is something you may want to mention to Lisa though."

"Oh, what's that?" Paige leaned forward, curious to hear what Violet had to say.

"Do you know Nancy Noggan?" Paige recognized the time and tried to picture who she was and then it came to her. Stylish woman in her late forties or maybe early fifties, it was hard to know for sure, but she was tall and lean, a runner maybe with toned arms. She had highlighted blonde hair that fell to her collar bone and big blue eyes.

"I know who she is," Paige said.

"Well, I think she's set her sights on Rhett and even though people have told her he's with Lisa, she seems to ignore it and flirts outrageously with him every time she goes in. And she's been going in more often lately. She's been at the bar every time I've been in over the past month or so. And Rhett seems to be giving her more attention than he used to. I'm not saying there's anything there, but if I were Lisa, I'd want to know about it."

"Hmmm. I will let her know. We haven't been into the restaurant in ages, maybe it's time Lisa and I went in for a drink and a bite to eat at the bar."

Violet smiled. "That's what I would do."

LISA CHECKED her outfit in the mirror and twirled to see how it looked from all angles. She'd lost five pounds since she got sick, and even though she could stand to lose fifteen more, she was feeling pretty good and her stomach looked a little flatter. She wore dark dressy jeans and her favorite pale blue cotton sweater with a flattering scooped neckline. She was finally feeling like herself again. She'd finished her course of antibiotics a few days ago and was back to her morning walks along the beach. But she made sure not to walk in any grassy areas.

She heard Paige's car pull into the driveway and met her outside and climbed into the passenger seat.

"You didn't tell him we're coming in, did you?"

Paige asked. Lisa was going to, but Paige insisted it was better not to, so he'd be just acting the way he normally would. Lisa didn't think that was necessary but after talking to Harry, she agreed to go along with what Paige suggested. Harry didn't think there was anything to it, but thought it might be good for Lisa to see for herself. She also thought it would be good for her just to get out after being cooped up at home recuperating. Lisa really wasn't concerned about Rhett. She knew in her heart that things were good with them. But she was curious to see this other woman in action and they hadn't been into the restaurant in ages.

They arrived at a quarter to six, early enough that there were still plenty of seats at the bar, but it was starting to fill up. Rhett was nowhere to be seen when they walked in and Lisa guessed he was in the kitchen talking to the chef. Paige led the way to the bar and made a beeline toward two empty seats, which happened to be next to Nancy Noggan. She was there in what Lisa guessed was her usual spot, the last seat on the end, near where the waitstaff came to pick up their drinks and where she'd see people coming and going out of the kitchen.

Just as they were about to sit, Nancy got up and headed off towards the rest rooms. Paige sat and left the empty seat, the one next to Nancy for Lisa.

"She doesn't know you, does she?" Paige asked.

"No, we've never met, so I don't think so."

"Good. You'll be able to hear her better by sitting there then."

"I'm not so sure this is a good idea," Lisa said. She was starting to second guess Paige's suggestion to visit the restaurant.

"Don't be silly! It's harmless and we haven't gone out in ages or come here, so it's all good."

As soon as they were seated, the bartender, a young woman that Lisa hadn't seen before, came over with a big smile and asked what they'd like to drink. They both went with white wine. A few minutes later, Nancy returned, sat down and didn't even glance their way. She picked up her martini and sipped it while she scanned the restaurant and her eyes lit up when she saw Rhett walk through the kitchen door. She smiled and waved him over.

"Quick, turn towards me," Paige whispered.

Lisa turned so her back was to Rhett and that woman.

"Good, he hasn't seen us. I can see and you can listen."

"This is silly," Lisa protested and went to turn around.

"Just wait a few minutes," Paige insisted.

"You look lovely tonight, Nancy," Rhett said in his usual charming way. Lisa didn't think anything of it, because he was like that with everyone.

"Thanks, Rhett. Say, you know, I was thinking about you earlier today. I remembered you said you love scallops and that you had some beauties in for a special the other night. Well, I heard there's a scallop festival downtown next weekend. If you're not busy, maybe we should check it out. I hear it's fantastic."

"Oh, my god!" Paige whispered. "The nerve of her."

"Shhhh," Lisa said. She wanted to hear Rhett's response.

"That sounds wonderful Nancy. Maybe we'll see you there. My Lisa loves scallops too and she mentioned going to the festival as well."

"You did?" Paige whispered.

"No, but it does sound good."

"Oh, I didn't realize things were serious with what's her name? Linda?"

Lisa fought back a giggle and turned towards Nancy and Rhett. He laughed when he saw her and to her delight, came over and planted a big kiss on her lips. From the corner of her eye, Lisa registered a look of dismayed shock on Nancy's face. It was quite satisfying to see.

"This is a nice surprise. I didn't realize you two were coming in."

"It was a last-minute thing. Paige was craving seafood."

Rhett turned back to Nancy and still had his arm around Lisa's shoulders.

"Nancy, I'd like you to meet Lisa Hodges, the woman I live with." He winked at Lisa and she smiled back. "Nancy is one of our regulars."

"Nice to meet you, Nancy."

Nancy looked as though she was anything but pleased to be meeting Lisa. "You as well," she said tightly and picked up her martini glass.

"What are you ladies in the mood for tonight?" Rhett said.

"I'm suddenly craving scallops," Lisa said.

"Me too," Paige said.

"Well, you won't be disappointed. No one does them like we do."

"That's what I hear." Lisa gave his arm a squeeze and he kissed her again.

Nancy took the final sip of her martini, pulled her bar tab from the cup in front of her and counted out cash to pay her bill and set it on the bar.

"Are you leaving us already, Nancy?" Rhett said.

"I'm tired. It's been a long day. Goodnight." She left and as soon as she was out the door, Rhett said,

"You really have no idea how glad I am that you came in tonight."

"You're very popular. Should I be worried?" Lisa teased him.

"You have nothing to worry about. You never will," he assured her.

18

Kristen ran into Tyler soon after talking to her sister. They both went to get their mail at the same time and before she could chicken out, she invited him to come to her cookout and pitch party Friday night. He looked like he'd been holed up writing for hours, maybe even a few days as he looked exhausted and badly needed a shave. Though the dark stubble shadow looked good on him. She guessed he'd been locked in the zone when time ceased to exist.

"I didn't expect to see anyone. Hope my appearance doesn't scare you. When the writing is going well, I forget to do basic things like bathe and shave."

Kristen laughed.

"You don't have to explain or apologize to me. I get

it. Kate too. In fact, my sister is dying to talk writing with you and pitch is more fun if we have four people. I can't promise the food will be good though. I'm just grilling burgers and dogs, but Kate's bringing her famous clam dip."

"Kate's clam dip? How can I say no to that? I haven't played pitch though. Is it hard?"

"No, we can teach you. It's just high, low, jack, game, you get a point for each and you can bid up to 4 points if you think your hand is really good and then everyone has to follow your suit. It's really fun. We can do a few practice rounds until you feel comfortable with it."

"I'm in. What time and what can I bring?"

"Just bring yourself. I think they're coming around six-thirty."

Tyler grinned. "All right then. I'm looking forward to it. I'll even shower and shave."

KRISTEN RAN out Friday morning to do her shopping for the cookout. She bought a box of Bubba burgers, some deli hot dogs, potato salad and on the way home, she stopped by Bradford liquors for wine and a six-pack of O'Doul's beer for Tyler. Peter Bradford smiled when he saw her.

"Hi Kristen, how's your mother feeling?" He asked and then added, "Paige told me she was fighting Lyme disease."

Kristen had heard from her mother that Paige and Peter were spending time together. By the smile on his face when he mentioned Paige's name, it seemed to be going well.

"She's doing much better, thanks. How's your kitten doing? I hear Paige adopted her brother?"

"She's great. Bundle of energy. You should get one."

Kristen laughed. "I could picture a kitten having a ball clawing my paintings."

"Hmmm, yeah, maybe not such a good idea then." He rang her up and handed her back her change.

"Thanks, Peter!"

KATE AND JACK arrived a little before six thirty and Kristen had the grill just about heated up. She put the burgers and dogs on and then happily let Jack take over keeping an eye on them while she got everything else they needed, rolls and condiments and Kate set out the chips and dip.

Tyler was right on time at six thirty and surprised Kristen by bringing her a bottle of La Crema

Chardonnay and a box of cannoli pastries from Mrs. Harvey's Bakery. Kristen was impressed.

"Thank you. That's actually my favorite chardonnay."

"So, I hear. The owner of Bradford's liquors suggested it. I'm clueless about wine. I was going to get some O'Doul's too, but he said you already had some. So, I stopped and picked up the cannoli too."

"You didn't need to, but it was very thoughtful. Thank you." Kristen put the cannoli into the refrigerator to keep the sweet cheese filling cold, opened the wine, pouring a glass for herself and Kate and got a cold O'Doul's for Tyler.

The sunset was gorgeous and the weather warm and breezy so they decided to eat outside. Kristen had an old picnic table that she'd picked up at a yard sale earlier in the summer and they ate there and chatted easily until the temperature dropped as the sun lowered and almost disappeared. They went inside then and Kate got a deck of cards from her purse and they sat around the small round table in Kristen's kitchen.

It didn't take long for Tyler to get the hang of playing pitch and they played for several hours, breaking halfway through to sample the cannoli. Jack and Tyler were chatting like old friends and discovered they shared a love for fishing.

Kate glanced at Kristen and laughed. "I really think it's a guy thing. Sitting for hours on a boat and odds are only fifty-fifty that you'll catch anything. Yet, they love it."

"It's no different from spending hours on the beach," Jack said. "That bores me to tears, but most girls love it."

Kristen smiled. "What's not to love? We usually chat for hours and read stacks of trashy magazines and eat junk food."

Kate peppered Tyler with questions about his writing process. He didn't seem to mind though and Kristen was glad to see that he was encouraging. She knew as a new writer that Kate struggled with finding her way and feelings of self-doubt.

"It never goes away," he said. "I start each book wondering if I'll be able to do it again or if it was all a fluke and I should give up and do something else. But somehow, it all comes together in the end. You have to get to the end, that's the key."

Kate nodded, and Kristen could tell she appreciated all of his advice.

"Do you find it easier to write here? Or do you miss Manhattan?" Kate asked.

"There are things I miss about Manhattan, definitely. There's always a buzz of energy there. So many people. It's funny though, I felt more alone there, even surrounded by all those people than I do here."

"What do you mean?" Kristen was intrigued by his comment.

"Just that here, I can be alone, hunker down and write and no one will bother me. But if I go into town, go to the liquor store for example, the owner will chat with me and will know the people I'm meeting with. Everyone seems to know everyone here. I'm sure that's not always a good thing, but I'm kind of liking it so far."

"He recognized you as a famous writer you mean?" Kate asked.

Tyler laughed. "No, not at all. He just remembered me as the guy that buys non-alcoholic beer and that was having dinner with people he knew."

Kate smiled. "I guess we take that for granted here. But, I know what you mean. I loved living in Boston, when I worked at the magazine. It's great to be right in the heart of a city too, but I was always a little home-sick for Nantucket." She looked at Jack and added, "The best thing that happened to me was getting laid off from Boston Style. Though I didn't see it at the time."

"Mom always says, 'everything happens for a reason'," Kristen said.

"There's definitely some truth to that," Kate agreed.

"All right, are we ready to dive in for another round?" Jack asked. "We could bet a dollar a round to make things interesting. Although, I'm warning you ahead of time, that I'm feeling lucky so prepare to lose your dollar."

They played three more rounds and Kate was actually the lucky winner of all three but by the end of the third round, she couldn't hold back the yawns and she and Jack decided to call it a night. Jack and Tyler exchanged numbers as Jack was eager to go fishing possibly over the weekend.

Once they left, Kristen's house felt oddly quiet. She looked at Tyler and he smiled slowly and the air shifted as a chill danced across her skin, and her senses were suddenly on high alert.

"We should probably exchange numbers too," Tyler suggested. "Since we're neighbors and all."

"In case I want to go fishing?" Kristen teased.

Tyler stepped towards her and reached a hand toward her face and she sucked in her breath as he brushed her hair off her face.

He chuckled, "That wasn't exactly what I had in mind."

She took a step closer to him and reached for a pen and paper on the counter. "What did you have in mind?" She meant for the words to come out teasingly, but instead there was a breathy quality to her voice and she wondered where that came from.

He closed the distance between them and looked into her eyes for a moment, looking for an answer to his unspoken question. Her eyes answered his and he smiled and brought his lips to hers. His kiss woke up all her senses. He kept it brief and went to pull back and end the kiss, but she wasn't ready for it to end, and she leaned into him. He responded by putting his arms around her and pulling her close. The kiss went on a bit longer until they both took a break and looked at each other in surprise.

"I didn't plan on doing that tonight," Tyler said.

"I didn't expect that you would. But, I'm glad that you did."

"Are you ready for something? For this? It hasn't been long since you were almost engaged." Tyler looked at her intently.

"It's funny, I swore off dating for a while, after Sean. I thought I needed a break and I wasn't in any hurry to get back out there. But then you showed up, and it feels right. I'd like to explore this, and just take it slowly if that works for you?"

"It does. Slow is good with me as I'm still settling in here. Maybe you can show me around, your favorite places?"

"I'd love that." Kristen jotted her number down on a scrap of paper, ripped it in half and handed the pen to Tyler, who did the same, then handed it back to her and gave her another slow sweet kiss before heading home.

19

Ryan never really had a chance. He was a great guy, and if Chase was still with Lauren, maybe she would have tried harder to find that elusive spark. But when they were sitting in that pub and Chase told her it was over with Lauren, Beth would have given anything to stay there with him. But, she left and went on the date with Ryan, and it was fine, but he wasn't Chase. And Ryan clearly sensed that she wasn't feeling it. She felt badly about that, but Beth was done trying to force something that wasn't obviously there. Especially when maybe, finally it seemed as though she might actually have a chance with Chase. Maybe he was finally seeing her differently.

Ryan didn't even try to kiss her goodnight this time. They had a perfectly nice dinner, but her thoughts were elsewhere and he'd ended the night by giving her a friendly hug and the suggestion to call him if she wanted to get together again. They both knew that wasn't going to happen and she felt a little guilty at the sight of his sad smile before he turned to walk to his car.

But Beth hardly slept that night. She was too excited to see Chase the next day, to see where things might go. She dressed more carefully than usual, put on a hint of makeup, not so much that anyone would notice but just enough so her lashes were a bit darker, her cheeks a little rosier, and she wore her favorite navy top, the one that made her hair look the color of a burning flame.

When Chase came into the office as usual around four, he smiled and asked how her day went and then he asked the question she was waiting for.

"So, how'd date number two go? Is this one a keeper?" He was leaning against the counter in front of her desk and as he smiled, there was a hint of mischief in his eyes.

She took a deep breath. "Not a keeper. I had to toss him back in the water. He's a nice guy though."

Chase looked surprised. "Oh, that's too bad. It looked like you were getting along great the other night at The Chicken Box."

"Abby says I'm too picky."

"That's not a bad thing. She says it to me too." He grinned. "We make a great pair, don't we?" He picked up his stack of mail and headed into his office.

"Yeah, we do," Beth said softly and turned back to her computer. Chase hadn't seemed as interested by her news as she'd hoped. The vibe from the other night was gone. Although maybe it was never there, maybe she'd imagined it, and saw something there that didn't exist because she wanted it so badly.

And maybe she was being impatient. After all, she just told him it was over with Ryan. What did she expect? That he'd profess undying love and they'd run off together. She knew she needed to give it more time and see if maybe there could be something there.

A month later, after taking more care with her appearance than usual and going out for after-work drinks with Chase every week, Beth was beyond frustrated. She also wondered if her mind was playing tricks on her. More than once she'd gotten that vibe, a flicker of what seemed like interest from Chase, both in the office as he teased her and over drinks when hours would pass and they'd laugh and commiserate over the fact that Lauren's confirmed new boyfriend Troy had indeed joined forces with David Wentworth and was going to be building his condos. Chase didn't regret passing on the project, but he didn't like all the attention Troy was getting as if he was the new hot thing on the island.

The final straw came when he got a text message from his friend Jim while they were out and he made a face at it, which made Beth ask about it.

"Jim wants to set you up with a single friend of his."

"He does? Is he good-looking?" She teased him, expecting him to discourage her. But he did the opposite.

"He is, and he's a good guy. Maybe you should go out with him."

"You really think that's a good idea?" She wanted him to say no.

"Why not? You're single, he's single? No reason not to, right?"

And just like that, the mood was broken. They'd been having such a good night. She'd thought that maybe finally, something might happen between them. And now she realized it never would.

"I'll think about it. I'm not really keen on fix-ups. I'm kind of tired too. I think I'm ready to head home."

When she got home, she cried buckets. Beth wasn't a crier normally and it was like she'd saved up a year's worth of good cries. It took her a long time to get to sleep but by the time she drifted off, she had formulated a plan.

SOMETHING WAS GOING on with Beth, and Chase couldn't figure out what it was. She wasn't her usual fun self and out of the blue, she asked to take two days off at the end of the week to visit a college friend that lived on the Cape. She had the vacation time coming, so he didn't care about that, but he missed their Friday night after-work drinks—it had become a new habit he'd gotten used to. And the office seemed empty without her there for those two days.

He'd been thinking about Beth a lot lately and his feelings were confusing. They'd been friends for years now and she'd worked for him for the past three. He'd never thought of her as anything other than a friend, but lately, he'd found himself considering the possibility, wondering if maybe there could be something there. But, he wasn't sure how she felt. Sometimes he sensed a hint of interest but then the moment would pass and one of them would make a joke and the moment would be gone.

He was also hesitant to go there until he was really sure of his feelings and of hers. He didn't want to ruin a good friendship or jeopardize their working relationship. Beth was his right hand, he needed her in the office. Did he need her outside of it too? What if she didn't want that or if he decided that he didn't after they'd already started something up? The best thing, the safest thing, would be to do nothing. To keep things exactly the way they were.

The following week, that Friday, when he'd been assuming they'd go for their usual after-work drinks, Beth instead asked if he had a moment to talk when he walked into the office. He knew that nothing good ever came from a conversation that started that way.

"Sure. Of course, what's up?" He leaned against her desk and smiled, hoping to warm up the chill that seemed to hang in the air.

"There's no easy way to say this, so I'm just going to say it. I'm leaving, moving off-island. I was offered a position in Chatham, for another builder. It seems like a good opportunity, and as much I've loved working for you, I need more. I mean, I think it's time for me to see what else is out there. To meet new people."

"Oh! Wow. I didn't know you were thinking of moving." Chase was stunned. He didn't see this coming, at all.

"I wasn't, but I think it's been a long time coming.

It's just time. I've lined up a temp for you, Marie is going to start on Monday, and I'll train her during my last two weeks here so you won't miss me at all, hopefully."

"I'll miss you." Chase couldn't imagine coming into the office and Beth not being there. But if this was what she wanted, and needed to do, he wanted to support her.

"I don't want you to go. But if this is what you want, I'll support your decision."

"It's what I need to do and I appreciate you understanding."

"I don't really, but you have to do what you have to do." Chase had no interest in living off-island and he didn't think Beth did either. She'd always talked about how much she loved Nantucket. But if she didn't want to be there, and didn't want to work for him anymore, there wasn't much he could do about that.

The next two weeks went by too fast. Marie started as Beth had said she would and she seemed nice enough. She was an older woman, about his mother's age and Beth did a good job training her. The office already felt differently though and he hated that. He insisted on taking Beth out for a final after work drink on her last Friday but it didn't feel the same. Even though she laughed as usual at his bad jokes and they talked about anything and everything like always, it was different, she was more distant, as if she was already pulling away from Nantucket, and from him.

He insisted on paying the tab, like he usually did and when they left, he gave her a longer, tighter hug and kissed the top of her head.

"I am going to miss you. Please keep in touch. If you decide you hate it there, you can always come back."

"Thanks, Chase. But I don't think I can come back."

Saying goodbye to Chase was even harder than she'd imagined it would be. Beth had thought she was all cried out after her epic night of crying a few weeks prior, but she surprised herself by how long and hard she cried before finally falling into a troubled sleep.

She had a reservation on the slow boat, the one that took vehicles on it, the next day in the late afternoon, and she'd promised Abby she'd stop by to see her before she left. She went over to her house mid-morning and Abby had her front door opened before she even got out of her car.

"I was listening for your car. Come on in, I just made a pot of cinnamon coffee." She poured some for both of them, added a pile of sugars to hers and offered the sugar to Beth when she was done.

"I just drink it black."

"You'd think I'd know that by now. Let's go sit." Abby led the way into the living room and they got comfortable on her plush sofas.

"Are you sure you want to do this? It's not too late to change your mind. Chase is devastated, and so am I. I'm going to miss you so much."

"I'm sure Chase is far from devastated. He'll be fine. I will miss you though. But I'm only going to Chatham. It's just a ferry ride away. I'll come visit."

"You'd better. You really think this is what you need to do?" Abby looked curious as if she was trying to figure out why Beth was going.

"I do. There's not enough here for me. I want what you and Jeff have and I don't think I'm going to find it here. And I'm going to be smarter about relationships and not hope for something that is never going to be there."

"What do you mean? Who are you talking about?"

But Beth didn't want to talk to Abby about Chase. That was too close for comfort. "Oh, it's nothing. There was someone I was interested in and I thought maybe he was interested but it never went anywhere and I invested too much time in hoping and waiting and I don't want to waste any more time."

Abby looked like she was going to say something but instead she just nodded. "You have to follow your gut. Do what you think is best. Selfishly though, I hope you might just get this out of your system and come back."

Beth felt her eyes water suddenly as the emotions she'd been trying to disregard made their way to the surface.

"I'll be back for your shower in a few months. I can't wait for that," Beth said.

"Well, I hope to see you sooner than that, but if I don't, we'll be in touch. Call me, Facebook me. I'll be here."

A week later, Beth was settled in Chatham. She was staying in her friend's guest cottage for the time-being until she found a more permanent year-round rental. The people at her new job were nice. It was a larger office and there was a receptionist as well as a book-keeper. Beth's role as office manager was to oversee them and to support the two brothers that owned the company. They were talented builders and completely different personalities and between the two of them they kept her very busy. So busy that she didn't have time to miss Chase.

That came when she went home at night and was by herself. Her friend Jane was happily married and they did things together, but Beth had a lot of alone time and it was hard not to think of Chase and to wonder how he was doing and if he was missing her.

20

Chase was a mess. In the two weeks that Beth had been gone, he hadn't slept well and was generally miserable. He missed her more each day. He realized how he'd taken for granted that she'd always be there in the office and that seeing her at the end of the day was what he looked forward to more than anything else. Marie was doing a fine job, Beth had trained her after all, but she wasn't Beth.

But what shook him to his core, was how much he missed her, not just her being in the office but just Beth herself. He missed spending his Friday nights with her. It was like a part of him was missing. The realization shocked him and made him doubt himself. How could he have taken so long to understand this? He still questioned if it was real and his biggest worry was that it was completely one-sided. Surely, if Beth had any kind of feelings for him, she wouldn't have left, would she?

He closed his eyes, imagining Beth's face, her hair, that color that was so unique to her, like a light-filled, flickering flame, and her lips. When she wore that one lipstick, her favorite one, it made her lips pinker and he regretted that he'd never had the chance to kiss them. He worried that he was losing his mind and was imagining something that wasn't there at all. As usual, when he needed to sort things out, he called his sister Abby.

"What are you doing?" He asked when she answered the phone, Saturday morning.

"Eating leftover cake for breakfast. What about you?"

"Feeling like visiting my baby sister, if she's not too busy?"

"Come on over."

A half hour later, he was sprawled across Abby's living room sofa while she sat on the love seat looking at him with concern.

"So, what's bothering you? Clearly something is on your mind."

"Well, I wanted to run something by you. It might sound a little crazy."

"I'm okay with crazy. Spill it."

"Well, I really miss Beth," he began.

"I know, so do I. Something awful. Is the woman

she found for you doing an okay job? I know you were so used to having Beth there."

"Oh, Marie's fine. It's not that. It's just, well, I miss Beth. More than I expected to."

Abby sat up straighter. "Really? You don't mean just working for you? Was there ever something between the two of you?"

"Between me and Beth? No, we've only ever been friends. But, I think, well I know, that I'm an idiot for not trying for something more. We've spent a lot of time together and I just really miss her."

"That's so interesting. Did you ever think about asking her out? Do you think she would have said yes?"

"It only recently crossed my mind, after Lauren and I broke up and I started to see her in a new light. But I wasn't sure of my feelings and I like her too much as a friend and an employee to screw that up. And then she left anyway, so I don't know. Maybe I should have just gone for it. Did she ever say anything to you?"

"About being interested in you? No. But, there was someone she was interested in. She said she was fooling herself that he was interested and she wasn't going to waste her time waiting around." Abby thought for a moment. "Her leaving felt really sudden. Did you guys have any kind of a disagreement? Did anything happen?"

"No! We never disagreed. I've been going over it,

too, trying to figure it out. The last conversation we had, before everything changed, was at the pub. Jim texted me asking if Beth was single. He wanted to set her up with a friend of his."

Abby narrowed her eyes. "Did you tell her this? Did you give her the impression that you thought this was a good idea? Please tell me you didn't do that."

"I might have said something like that."

"Chase, you are an idiot. You do realize she probably heard that loud and clear as 'I am not interested in you, go out with someone else.'"

"Oh. You really think so?"

Abby nodded and Chase saw frustration and sympathy in her eyes.

"I really am an idiot," he agreed.

"So, what are you going to do about it?"

Chase grinned. "I guess I need to go check the ferry schedule."

CHATHAM HAD ALWAYS BEEN one of Beth's favorite towns on Cape Cod. It reminded her a little of Nantucket with its pretty Cape style house, lush lawns and beautiful beaches. On the weekends, she'd been enjoying exploring her new town and loved to go on long walks, taking pictures of the lighthouses and all the seals sunning themselves on the rocks. There were so many seals all over the Cape now that great white shark sightings had become a daily occurrence in the summer months, but she hadn't seen a shark yet.

It was almost four in the afternoon when she made her way back to her cottage. She'd had a good walk, almost an hour and she was ready for a hot shower and maybe a Hallmark movie. As she got closer though, she saw a familiar looking truck in her driveway. It couldn't be though. It must be a friend of Jane's or her husband. But then the truck door opened and Chase stepped out and took a step towards her.

"Hi Beth." He grinned, but he didn't seem as sure of himself as he usually did.

"Chase! What are you doing here?" She gave him a hug and he squeezed her tight and then let go.

"Would you believe I was just in the neighborhood?" He teased.

She laughed. "Right. Seriously, why are you here?"

Chase took a breath. "This is harder than I thought it would be," he began. "This might sound crazy, if you're not feeling the same way that I am, but I just had to know. Do you have feelings for me? Is that why you left?"

Beth didn't say anything. She didn't know what to say. Chase took her hands and pulled her a little closer to him and looked deeply into her eyes. When he spoke again, his voice shook a little, "Here's the thing. I miss you, more than I ever imagined that I would. It's just not the same without you there."

"Marie's not doing a good job?" Beth was confused at first.

He smiled. "It's not Marie. I just miss you. I miss you in the office. I miss going for Friday drinks with you. Since you've left, I've realized that I don't just miss you as a friend. I want more than that. A lot more."

Beth held her breath. It was hard to believe that the words she'd always longed to hear were finally being said. She was scared to trust it.

"How do I know you mean this? That it's not just a fleeting feeling? Until something better comes along? I don't want to ruin our friendship."

"I don't either. I wanted to ask you out weeks ago when I felt something shift, but I didn't trust it then. I'll admit that I wasn't sure enough of my feelings and I didn't want to hurt you ever, if I didn't see it going anywhere. You mean too much to me, as a friend and as an employee."

"But you feel differently now?" Beth felt the flicker of hope expand.

"Let me show you." Chase pulled her closer and brought his lips down to hers and he showed her. To say there were sparks was an understatement.

"Okay, you've convinced me."

"Come home, Beth. Come back to Nantucket. Come back to work for me and let's just be together. We can take it as slow or as fast as you want. I'm yours, however you want me. If you want me, that is?" He looked a little unsure and Beth laughed, put her arms around his neck and drew him down to her.

"I want you," she whispered, and then she showed him how much.

CHASE STAYED OVER THAT NIGHT. They walked down to Main Street and had a wonderful dinner at the Impudent Oyster and then walked over to the Chatham Squire to listen to some live music. It was the most magical night that Beth could remember. They stayed up until the wee hours of the night, talking, and laughing and kissing.

When she woke the next morning, she wondered at first if it had all been a dream. But then she saw Chase still sleeping peacefully and her heart swelled.

She gave her notice that Monday, worked her two weeks and moved home to Nantucket that Saturday. She and Chase were inseparable and two weeks after she moved home, he surprised her on Friday when they were having a beer at their favorite pub.

"Why don't you give up your place for good and move in with me?"

"Really? You don't think it's too soon?"

He leaned over and kissed her before saying, "You're over most nights anyway and I miss you when you're not there."

"All right. I'll move in." It felt right and Beth finally knew to trust her gut.

21

The night before Thanksgiving

Abby and Kristen arrived at Kate and Jack's house a little before seven. Abby had a bag of apples and two cans of pumpkin puree. Kristen had a bottle of chardonnay, French onion dip and a bag of ruffled chips. Kate happily took the bottle from her when they walked through the door. They followed her to the kitchen and set everything on the counter. Kate poured the wine while Kristen tore open the bag of chips and Abby settled herself on one of the chairs facing the island.

"I'm sorry I can't offer you wine, but I have a nice herbal tea," Kate offered her.

"Sure, that sounds good. I can make it if you like." Abby started to get up.

"Sit and relax. I'll just throw a cup of water in the microwave." Kate handed a glass of wine to Kristen and got the pre-made pie crusts out of the fridge.

"Where's Jack?" Kristen asked. "I thought he'd be here."

Kate laughed. "He heard you were both coming over to bake pies and he decided to get out of the way. He went out for pizza and beers with his brother and I think a few others." She handed Abby her hot tea when it was ready and a bowl of sugar. They all knew her sweet tooth was out of control these days.

Like they did every year, the girls got together the night before Thanksgiving to make apple and pumpkin pies. Their mother took care of the rest, the turkey and all the side dishes. They were going to have a bigger group than usual this year. Rhett and his daughter Michelle were joining them, as well as Beth and Chase. Everyone approved of Beth, she was a huge improvement over Lauren and Kate had a feeling, since they'd been happily living together for a few months, that they might be the next to announce an engagement. Though she supposed the rest of the family might think that about her and Jack too. They'd casually talked about marriage once or twice but Kate didn't feel any urgency to get engaged. She was happy living with Jack and it seemed like they were in a good place.

"How are things going with Tyler?" She asked Kristen. One never knew with Kristen how things were going in her relationships as she didn't talk much about it. But she seemed mostly happy since they'd started dating. Kate liked Tyler. She only wondered sometimes if they might be too much alike, two moody artists, both lost in their heads for much of the day. And she worried a little about Tyler being an alcoholic. As far as she knew, he hadn't had any issues but if he did, that would be hard to deal with.

"Up and down, mostly up," Kristen said. "I've never dated another artist before and it's interesting. We have so much in common, but we can both be kind of introverted and moody. It's not usually a problem, but sometimes, when Tyler is distant or stressed out, I worry that something else is going on, that he might relapse."

"Has he since you've been dating?" Abby asked.

"No. And it's probably nothing to worry about. We just haven't really been tested yet, nothing too stressful has happened to either one of us. It will probably never be an issue."

"Have you ever thought about going to an Al-Anon meeting? I don't know much about it, but maybe you could find some support?" Kate suggested.

"Funny you mention that. I actually just went to my first meeting last week. I wanted to find out what it was all about and maybe just get some information, so I'll know what to do, just in case he ever falls off the wagon. I'm probably being a nervous Nellie, but I did feel better after I went."

"I think that was smart," Abby said.

"This is actually the first glass of wine I've had in a while." Kristen smiled. "It tastes really good. Though I feel a little guilty that Tyler can't enjoy it."

"You don't drink around him?" Kate thought that was interesting. Tyler didn't seem to have a problem being around others who were having a glass or wine or beer.

"I did at first, but if it's just the two of us, I'll usually have something non-alcoholic. I've been drinking a lot of tea." She smiled. "To be honest, I don't really miss it. But I do enjoy it when we get together and I'm sure I'll have one of Mom's mimosas tomorrow."

"How are you feeling, Abby?" Kristen asked as her sister reached for the chips and dip.

"Fat. I'm feeling fat. I want this baby out." She laughed as she scooped a pile of dip onto her chip.

"It won't be much longer. I wonder if you'll actually have the baby on Christmas?" Kristen said. Abby's due date was December 25.

"Would you want that birthday?" Kate asked.

"I knew a kid who was born on December 26. She said it was a horrible day, being so close to Christmas because everyone forgot about her, or gave her the combo gift, 'oh, by the way this is for your birthday too'. But, no matter what day it is, we'll make sure to make a big fuss. Maybe we'll celebrate half birthdays too, so it feels like a separate special day." Abby absent-mindedly rubbed her belly. "She's been kicking a lot lately. I think she's anxious to get out too."

"I can't wait to meet her," Kate said.

"Me too. Have you decided on a name yet?" Kristen asked.

"We're torn between two, Natalie and Sophie. I think when we meet her, we'll know."

"Maybe she'll be late and be a New Year's Eve baby. Now that would be a fun birthday," Kate said.

Abby laughed. "It would. But something tells me she's not that patient."

Kristen opened the bag of apples and got a big bowl that that she lined with paper towels. She set the apples and bowl on the island counter between Abby and Kristen, then went to a kitchen drawer and returned with three peelers. She handed one to each sister, then sat in the middle chair between them.

"Okay ladies, let's get peeling and pie-making."

22

Unlike the majority of people, Lisa Hodges never felt stressed about hosting Thanksgiving. She loved every minute of it, puttering around the kitchen all morning, chopping and mixing and stirring all the different side dishes and basting the turkey. As much as she loved to cook though, she didn't enjoy baking as much and was glad that the girls were making the pies. She'd bought the coffee cake that they all loved from the Boston Coffee Cake company and as usual, they'd have that with her famous mimosas, made with fresh-squeezed orange juice and a splash of champagne when everyone arrived around eleven thirty.

She got up a little earlier than usual that morning to get her beach walk in before bringing the breakfast items into the dining room. She only had a few rooms rented for the holiday, and her guests were all visiting nearby family for the big Thanksgiving meal, so she made lighter food than usual for them—an egg white frittata with peppers and asparagus and the usual assortment of breads, bagels and fresh fruit.

Rhett joined her for coffee and a bagel and seemed a little preoccupied. She wondered if he was worried about his daughter feeling comfortable around everyone. Michelle had arrived the night before and was staying in one of the upstairs guest rooms. Rhett wanted to pay for her room, but Lisa wouldn't hear of it. They weren't fully booked so it wasn't like she was losing money.

When they finished eating, Lisa dove back into getting things ready. She had just finished browning the sausage to add to her grandmother's stuffing recipe, when Rhett came up beside her with an odd look on his face.

"Can you take a little break and come into the living room for a minute?" He asked.

"Sure." She quickly washed her hands and went into the living room where Rhett was standing by the fireplace. He'd started a fire and it was glowing merrily. He took her hands and pulled her towards him and gave her a quick kiss. "Happy Thanksgiving." He had never struck her as overly sentimental before, but she went with it.

"Happy Thanksgiving. I'm glad you're here. And Michelle too."

"Before everyone gets here, I wanted a moment alone with you. To tell you that what I'm most grateful for this year....is you. Meeting you, and loving you was unexpected and I can't imagine not having you in my life."

His words were unexpected and Lisa felt a sudden rush of emotion followed by the arrival of happy tears that threatened to spill over.

"I feel the same way. Totally unexpected. I didn't think I'd find love again, it wasn't even on my radar. And then you showed up."

"And then I showed up." He reached into his pocket and then looked her in the eye. "I know we haven't really talked about this, other than that I'd like to stick around through the winter, but I'd actually like to stay a lot longer."

The tears spilled over as Rhett slowly got down on one knee and held a small, black velvet box in one hand. He opened it and the most lovely, perfect diamond ring sat there in a delicate, vintage setting.

"If you'll have me, that is. I love you, Lisa Hodges. What do you think about getting married?" And then he added, "to me." And she laughed.

"Honestly, I haven't thought about it. I've just been

enjoying our time together, taking each day as it comes. But, yes, of course I'll marry you."

"It's a good deal for you. If I move into the main house, you'll have an extra room to rent," he said, with a twinkle in his eye as he slid the ring onto her finger, then stood and kissed her.

"Well, then. I guess we really have something to celebrate today. And to be grateful for." A thought occurred to her. "Does Michelle know? Do you think she'll be okay with this?" Lisa didn't know Rhett's daughter well. She was the same age as Abby, and Lisa hoped that it wouldn't make her more uncomfortable to learn her father just got engaged.

Rhett grinned, which immediately relaxed her. "I cleared it with her first. She actually helped me pick out the ring yesterday. Well, I had this picked out, but wanted to make sure I hadn't screwed it up. So, they held it for me, and I brought her to look at it and she gave an enthusiastic approval. Do you think your children will be okay with it?"

"We'll find out soon enough."

A FEW HOURS LATER, everyone began to arrive. Abby made a beeline for the coffee cake and started cutting slices for everyone. Lisa was ready for a slice too. She took a quick bite, savoring the flavor of the toasted walnuts and cinnamon sugar before handing out mimosas to everyone. She handed one to Tyler that was minus the champagne, just all fresh-squeezed orange goodness. She handed Kate her drink last because she knew she was the observant one and wouldn't miss the glittering ring on her finger. No one else had noticed yet. She laughed when Kate's jaw dropped and before she could say a word, Rhett commanded everyone's attention and held up his glass.

"I have an announcement. Or rather, we do." He glanced at Lisa and she nodded for him to continue. "As most of you have noticed, Lisa and I have grown close since I moved in here. We both feel lucky to have found each other and well, this morning, I asked her to marry me, and she said yes. We hope that you'll all be happy for us."

Lisa looked around at all the stunned faces. "We have a lot to be grateful for and we're glad to share this day with all of you."

Michelle was the only one who didn't look surprised, since she was in on it, and she made the first move to give Lisa a hug. "Welcome to the family. My dad is crazy about you."

"Thank you. That means a lot." Lisa felt her eyes

getting wet again as there was a sudden rush of noise and hugs and laughter as all of her children rushed forward to hug and congratulate both Lisa and Rhett.

THE REST of the day was a happy blur. Later that afternoon, after they finished eating, the girls helped Lisa finish cleaning up in the kitchen. All day, they took turns admiring her ring.

"He really has good taste. That setting is so pretty. I love the vintage filigree," Beth said.

"Chase, are you paying attention?" Rhett said.

"What was that? I must have missed it." Chase grinned and pulled Beth in for a quick kiss.

Lisa was glad to see her son so happy, finally. All of her children seemed settled now, although Kristen and Tyler were still a new couple. She liked Tyler and she was optimistic about him for Kristen. She hoped that their relationship would grow stronger and that the niggling concern she felt was just a mother being silly and worrying about nothing.

"Did you hear that Olivia Stark died this morning?" Kate said. Olivia was an elderly woman that lived right up the road. She'd been one of their neighbors for as long as Lisa could remember. She knew that Olivia had been sick for some time though and hadn't lived at home now for a few months. The house was starting to show the neglect. A recent storm had whipped off some of the shingles.

"I saw that on Facebook this morning," Chase said. "She was a nice old lady. She must have been close to ninety?"

"Closer to ninety-five, I think," Lisa said. "She was a good neighbor. I always felt bad for her all alone there with no family that I ever knew of."

"I wonder what will happen to her house now?" Kristen said.

"I'm sure she has a will. If there's no family, she probably left it to charity or something," Lisa guessed.

"Whoever buys it will need to do some work to it. With all those missing shingles, I wouldn't be surprised at a minimum if it needs a new roof," Chase said.

"Well, she won't have to worry about that now." Lisa said a silent prayer for the woman, hoping that she was at peace.

"Oh my goodness!" Abby sounded breathless and a bit alarmed. Lisa glanced over and saw why. Abby was leaning against the kitchen counter staring down at the floor and a puddle of water beneath her.

Jeff ran over and took her arm. "What's wrong, are you okay?"

Lisa took charge. "Jeff get her out to the car. Her water just broke."

"But it's too early," he said.

"I told you she was impatient," Abby said. But then she grabbed onto her mother's arm and in a panicky voice asked, "It's not too early is it? Should I be worried?"

"No, it's not too early. Babies come early all the time. I had a feeling this one might be in a hurry." Lisa smiled and gave her daughter's hand a reassuring squeeze. "I was a month early with you too, so this doesn't surprise me at all. Let's get you to the hospital."

LATER THAT EVENING, well after midnight as she drifted off to sleep with Rhett's arm around her, Lisa thought about what a wonderful and eventful day it had been. And how when one door closed another one opened. Ninety-something Olivia Stark slipped away in the early morning and Natalie Ellis arrived in the late evening, and all was as it should be.

THANK you so much for reading! I hope you enjoyed Nantucket Neighbors. If you'd like to receive an email about new releases, please join my mailing list. Visit my website, www.pamelakelley.com

My next book, Nantucket White Christmas is available for preorder.

Made in the USA
Coppell, TX
21 May 2020

26261468R00150